Jessica —

She's still being a bitch!

Fanning the Flames

Lisa R. Schoolcraft

Fanning the Flames

Lisa R. Schoolcraft

Copyright © 2022 Lisa R. Schoolcraft

All rights reserved. This book or any portion thereof may not be reproduced or used in any manner whatsoever with the express written permission of the publisher, except for the use of brief quotations in a book review. This is a work of fiction. Names characters, places and incidents are either the products of the author's imagination or are used fictitiously. Any resemblance to actual persons, living or dead, businesses, companies, events or locales is entirely coincidental.

Printed in the United States of America

First Printing, 2022

ISBN-13: 978-1-7339709-6-9

Publisher: Schoolcraft Ink LLC

Visit the author's website at www.schoolcraftink.com

Table of Contents

Chapter 1 1
Chapter 2 9
Chapter 3 19
Chapter 4 28
Chapter 5 35
Chapter 6 45
Chapter 7 55
Chapter 8 64
Chapter 9 71
Chapter 10 79
Chapter 11 89
Chapter 12 100
Chapter 13 107
Chapter 14 111
Chapter 15 118
Chapter 16 129
Chapter 17 137
Chapter 18 137
Chapter 19 156
Chapter 20 165
Chapter 21 173
Chapter 22 184

Chapter 1

Laura Lucas drove along Peachtree Road in Buckhead, her car's sunroof opened to a beautiful early fall day, the sun shining down on her.

Atlanta was her city now. Her home. She headed toward her condo, but, as usual, traffic was heavy during Atlanta's rush hour, which started as early as two o'clock in the afternoon some days and ended much later in the evening.

She didn't care. Cocooned in her Mercedes-Benz, when Laura could move forward, she could feel the slight warm breeze through her thick black hair.

Laura finally felt like her old self. Her right wrist, broken earlier that summer when an arsonist had tried to kill her, had healed.

Laura rolled her wrist as she sat in traffic. The wrist still bothered her, but it was better, thanks to some good physical therapy, paid by the new health insurance provided by her new full-time job.

Even in the warmth of her car, Laura shuddered at the memory of that night in Napa Valley. Walker Folks, a farm hand who had set several fires at Star 1 winery, where she provided her public relations talents at the request of the winery's new owner. She'd walked in on Walker trying to set fire to the winery's office. He'd tried to trap her in there, attempting to set it, and her, on fire.

Laura often awoke in a cold sweat after dreaming of his menacing face as he told her to "Die, bitch." In the half shadows of that small office, his face looked evil. She could still hear him click his cigarette lighter. It had gone out as it sailed through the air. Miraculously, the gasoline-soaked room and her gasoline-soaked clothes did not ignite.

The miracle of that night almost made Laura, a lapsed Catholic, start praying again. Almost.

Laura shook the memories from her mind as she pulled into her condo's underground garage. Since she lived in the penthouse, she had her own personal parking spot, away from other residents.

She unlocked her door, then turned and set her security system — including the extra one she'd had installed without her condo association's knowledge or consent. It was expensive, but it meant she slept better at night.

Laura had recently started to work full-time for Kyle Quitman, CEO of Black Kat Investors. That summer she'd done contract work for Star 1, one of Quitman's investments, and proved she was worth her salt.

He'd agreed to hire her full-time to provide public relations for his other investments. Being his employee also meant healthcare coverage. Those several sessions of physical therapy on her wrist weren't cheap.

I guess nearly being killed on the job guilted Kyle into hiring me, Laura thought bitterly. But she was glad to be working steadily again.

The granddaughter of Cuban immigrants, Laura had always been proud of her good looks, her dark black hair, her deep brown eyes. She was also fiercely proud of always being able to stand on her own two feet, making her way in the world. Her father had paid for her to attend a small private women's college in Virginia.

A degree in communications, with an emphasis in public relations and marketing, allowed Laura to use her brain and her beauty.

A native of Miami, Laura had worked for several companies since she'd graduated from college in December 1994. She'd taken classes every summer so she could graduate early. She hadn't even invited her parents to graduation and skipped the ceremony herself.

Laura headed straight for Atlanta in early 1995 and worked for an advertising agency in the run-up to the 1996 Summer Games.

Hired to help hand out Olympic-sponsored merchandise on Atlanta city streets during the Games, Laura found she was good at sales, too.

Fanning the Flames

She was in demand, and she changed jobs often, getting better pay as she worked her way up the ladder.

Her youth, good looks and sex appeal didn't hurt. Neither did sleeping with the occasional married boss to get a promotion.

After nearly 10 years working for others, she'd gone into business for herself, juggling many clients, but focusing on the commercial real estate industry, which was booming when she'd started working for herself.

Then the Great Recession hit, and she struggled to make ends meet. Clients disappeared or couldn't and didn't pay. She still had a mortgage to pay.

Laura smiled when she thought about how she'd bought her condo in Buckhead at just the right time when the builder was going broke and was willing to sell it for well below its value. She'd asked her father to help with the loan, the only time she'd asked him for financial help after college.

Laura didn't like to admit it, but she had been struggling financially before getting hired by Kyle's Black Kat Investors. She'd blown through most of her savings on her mortgage, the car payment on her Mercedes, and the lifestyle she still wanted to live.

Kyle initially hired her to do publicity for the Napa winery in which he had a majority stake. In nearly getting killed by the psychotic arsonist, she'd gotten herself hired full-time.

Laura was willing to do whatever it took, work with whatever clients he wanted, to get back on her feet financially again.

She was still doing some publicity for Star 1, but she was glad to be doing it from Atlanta. She'd tangled with Bobby Pearce, the winery manager and former owner, over her ideas for the winery. Then she tangled under the sheets with the handsome man.

Bobby had wanted more from her, wanted her to stay in Napa with him. Laura couldn't be tied down to any man and was relieved when it was time for her to go.

Laura scheduled a meeting with Simon Beck, one of the partners in Seventh Heaven Restaurant Group, to go over the preliminary publicity for the new Italian restaurant, Buon Cibo, in Buckhead, a trendy part of

Atlanta. Kyle had bought into the partnership, bringing the total number of partners to four.

Kyle's investment allowed the partners to build a new restaurant on a corner of land near Lenox Square, one of the area's luxury malls.

Laura's head swam with ideas about the new restaurant. She'd already outlined how the restaurant's pre-launch should go, and how to build up a fan base before the launch using social media influencers.

She created several social media accounts for Buon Cibo, "Good Food" in Italian, including Instagram, Pinterest, Twitter, and a Facebook page, and planned to post lots of food photos ahead of the restaurant's opening.

She gathered the names of the top 10 social media influencers in Atlanta and planned to reach out to them to help her promote Buon Cibo. She hoped to invite them to lunch and have Simon create some menu items. She hoped they would post the food photos online, then rave about the food.

Laura wondered if she should get a new outfit for her meeting with Simon. Not that she didn't have plenty of lovely outfits in her closet. But something about a new dress made her feel more powerful and feminine at the same time.

Laura wandered the aisles of Neiman Marcus in Lenox Square but didn't find anything that suited her. Laura was a petite woman, and looked in the petite section, but nothing made her feel sexy and powerful, no matter what she tried on.

She drove back to her condo with a new Hermes handbag from the Buckhead Atlanta shopping center. That was as close as she was going to come to powerful and sexy for the day.

Laura realized she could afford the bag with the salary Kyle was now paying her. But she considered this part of the bonus he had promised when she delivered.

Kyle had offered Laura bonuses for increased sales and income. Laura was sure she could deliver. After all, hadn't she made Star 1 winery the most talked about winery in Napa Valley? That arson fire hadn't hurt. It had hurt Laura, but not the winery. Now Star 1 wines were in demand.

She even created campaigns playing off the fire: "Star 1. The hottest winery in Napa" and "Find out why our wines are on fire."

Fanning the Flames

Laura realized her bonus was likely part of the guilt Kyle felt over her arson injuries. But she'd show him and Simon Beck. She'd make Seventh Heaven Restaurant Group and Buon Cibo one of the top restaurant groups and names in Atlanta.

Laura rubbed her right wrist again as she grabbed the Hermes bag out of her Mercedes Benz. She walked into the lobby of Simon Beck's Midtown condo. She asked the concierge to let her up.

In the elevator, she prepared to meet Simon again after having met him years ago. He'd been married then. She knew he was separated now. She arched her eyebrow. Maybe there was a chance this could be a personal win for her.

Kyle had told her to keep her hands off his employees, but Simon Beck wasn't an employee. He was a partner in the restaurant group. That wouldn't violate their "don't sleep with the employees" agreement, would it?

Laura smiled as the elevator doors opened. She was sure it wouldn't.

Simon Beck greeted Laura at the front door of his condo. He gave her a quick tour of the living room and the kitchen. He left the bedrooms and bathrooms off the tour.

She walked in and was immediately impressed. From his living room balcony, she could see nearly into Piedmont Park. This was some serious real estate, Laura realized. She tried to hide her smile.

This is going to be fun, she thought to herself.

"Why are you smiling?" Simon asked.

Laura, caught in her reverie, quickly said, "I was just admiring your view. I love how close you are to Piedmont Park."

"Oh, do you go to Piedmont Park often?"

"Oh, never to exercise. I don't run or anything."

"But you look like you're in good shape."

"I never exercise outside, I mean. I do yoga every morning in my condo." That wasn't a complete lie. When she remembered, she did yoga. "And sometimes I throw in some Pilates. Those are indoors, though."

"I'm hoping to do some running in the park, but with the restaurant design and menu selection taking up so much of my time, I haven't gotten to enjoy it yet. I'm hoping I'll get to before my lease runs out."

"You are renting?"

"Yes. Until my wife and I figure out... Well, that's none of your business. Kyle said you will do publicity for Buon Cibo."

"Well, that's why I'm here. To help put together some pre-publicity on the restaurant and then help with the actual launch."

Simon offered her a seat at his kitchen island's breakfast bar. The kitchen was an open design. The island had an ice bucket with a Pinot Grigio chilling, two wine glasses, and a small charcuterie board, with olives, cheese, and prosciutto.

Laura could feel her mouth begin to water.

"Shall we?" Simon asked, reaching for the wine bottle. "I hope you like Pinot Grigio. My wine distributor sent over several Italian wines for me to try, to see what I might want to carry in the restaurant."

"So, this is research?"

"You could say that."

"Well, fill my glass. I like this kind of research."

Simon poured the straw-colored wine into her glass, then poured one for himself. He sniffed it, swirled it in his glass, then took a small sip. He held it in his mouth and breathed in. Then he swallowed.

"Not bad. Tell me what you think."

Laura tried to imitate what Simon had done but only sniffed it, then took a sip. "It is nice. It's very crisp."

"You are not doing it correctly," Simon snapped. "It's sniff, sip, swirl, swallow."

Simon repeated the process slowly, looking at Laura each time he did a step.

Abashed, Laura followed his instructions carefully.

"If you are going to be helping me with my publicity, I need you to do things correctly," he scolded. "You've got to know about food and wine."

Simon's demeanor then changed. He began speaking pleasantly.

"It should go very well with these," he said, pointing to the board with the charcuterie. "Especially that parmesan cheese."

Laura bristled at his outburst, and she was more careful in her conversations. She didn't realize she was dealing with a drama queen, or in his case, a drama king. She didn't remember him being so

Fanning the Flames

temperamental, but then maybe he was stressed out about opening the new restaurant.

They talked for several hours about Laura's ideas. Once they finished with the charcuterie, they moved to Simon's plush light gray sofa. The living room was done in neutrals, but the accent pieces were bold, like his bright gold framed mirror on the wall and gold lamp on the end table.

Simon had opened another bottle of the Pinot Grigio and sat across from Laura on the sofa.

"Your apartment really is lovely. Perhaps we can invite some of the social media influencers over for something like this. You know, small plates, a couple of bottles of this nice wine. Let them take photos and blast them out to their followers. That's a good way to create buzz about the new restaurant."

"How many are you going to invite? I don't want too many."

"No, we'd make it very exclusive. I'll look to see how many followers each has. Maybe only three or four. That will create some buzz too. Only the top influencers get this chef's table style treatment."

Laura's eyes were wide with excitement. She took a small notebook out of her new white and gold Hermes handbag and jotted notes down.

"Will you be here when this chef's table, as you call it, happens?"

"Of course. I'm not going to leave you hanging. I'll script the whole thing if you aren't sure about what to say."

"My wife — I mean my estranged wife — would never come to any sort of function at my restaurants. Didn't like the crowds. It's good to know you'll be working for me and help work the room."

"I work for Kyle," Laura said, testily. "That's what Kyle pays me for."

"Sure. Whatever." Simon waved his hand dismissively. "But at my event you work for me."

Laura looked up to see the street lights illuminated near the park. She stood up and placed her wine glass down on the island countertop.

"This has been lovely," she said. She didn't like the way he had begun to order her around. "I should be going. I didn't realize how late it had gotten."

"Are you OK to drive? I should have fixed you some dinner."

"I'm fine. But I will take you up on my own chef's table. I'll be honest. I'm looking forward to trying the menu. I really love Italian food."

"Have you been to Italy?"

"No. I'd love to go some time. If you decide to go there anytime soon, let me know and maybe we can talk Kyle into paying for it as a business expense."

"You forget. I'm one of the partners. I pay the bills, too. With the expense of this new restaurant, there will be no trip to Italy, or any other junket paid by this company. If I can't go, you can't go."

"Can't blame a girl for asking."

Relieved to be home, Laura entered her condo, tossed her keys in a ceramic bowl on a side table by the front door and kicked off her Jimmy Choo slingback heels. She put her Hermes bag carefully on the table.

Laura loved shopping. She considered it her true hobby. Hermes, Jimmy Choo, Gucci, Louis Vuitton. The retail clerks at the shops in Buckhead all knew her by name. It gave her a thrill to find a new trendy bag or shoe. She loved it.

Laura usually wore heels – the higher the better – since she was so petite. Laura needed the heels to give her slight frame a vertical boost.

Laura walked barefoot into her kitchen and opened the refrigerator. She didn't have much in there. She usually ate out and regretted that she didn't stop and get takeout on her way home from Simon's Midtown condo.

She reached for her phone to order delivery, then put the phone down. She wasn't sure what she wanted this evening. With all the talk of Italian food, she was thinking of ordering from Saint Cecilia, just down the road from her condo. But would that be disloyal to Simon's venture?

Laura justified eating at what would become a rival Italian restaurant as market research. Surely, she could expense the meal.

She picked up the phone and ordered a pasta dish and a side dish. She opened a bottle of chilled Chardonnay from her refrigerated wine cellar while she waited for her DoorDash to arrive.

Her condo's concierge called her to say her food had arrived and sent someone up to deliver it. She loved where she lived. The penthouse had its perks.

Chapter 2

Laura ended up drinking the entire bottle of Chardonnay. It wasn't the fancy wine Simon had served her last night, but it was just as good three glasses in.

Laura woke up the next morning slightly hungover, but strong Cuban coffee and a shower later, she was ready to greet the day.

She planned to reach out to some Instagram influencers. She was hoping she'd have to take a few of them to lunch at nice restaurants in Buckhead. A business expense if there ever was one. She'd turn in every receipt with the names of the influencers to Kyle's investment firm.

Laura reached out to Elaine Dennis, Valerie Tennell, and Maria Calas. All three responded that they were interested in the chef's table with Simon and would love to have lunch with Laura to talk about potential campaigns. All of them had at least 30,000 followers.

Laura smiled. It was like shooting fish in a barrel.

By mid-afternoon, Laura began to think about what she would do that evening. She might text Craig Dawson. He was a former commercial real estate client. She'd had an affair with him until he decided to go back to his wife to try to fix his marriage.

But he'd texted her recently that he'd like to see her again. Maybe the reconciliation with his wife wasn't going so well, Laura surmised.

She decided to text Craig back and see if he could meet her for dinner. She hoped it would lead to more than just dinner. She hoped it would lead to dessert. Dessert that ended up at her place.

Craig replied he would have to make an excuse about a business dinner. Could he meet her at an out-of-the-way restaurant? Maybe in Sandy Springs? He doubted his wife would have friends that frequented any restaurant in Sandy Springs.

Sandy Springs? Laura wasn't so sure about going outside the perimeter, or OTP, as those in Atlanta called it. She wanted a nice restaurant, somewhere in Buckhead. She texted back she wanted a nice place. What about somewhere in Midtown?

Craig asked if she could meet him at Oceanaire. He'd ask for a private area, somewhere in the back. Laura said she'd meet him there at eight o'clock.

Laura was excited to see Craig again. He was a good lover, attentive. And he was wealthy. If she started seeing him again, on the sly, she hoped he would send her lots of nice gifts. She could use a new Prada handbag. Her "old" one was last year's bag.

She could also use some good sex. Craig liked things a little rough. His wife was too vanilla, he'd said. He liked to do it doggy style, grabbing her breasts as he entered her from behind. He also liked anal sex.

Laura wasn't all that wild about anal sex, but Craig usually gave her a nice bauble afterward. She got a pair of diamond earrings from him once. She wore them on their date that night.

Laura ordered the most expensive thing on the menu, the filet mignon and crab cake with truffle whipped potatoes. She considered the lobster but decided on surf and turf.

She also ordered some oysters as appetizers. And they'd ordered a bottle of wine. Laura was pleased her meal cost well over $100. Laura wanted to be treated like a queen.

When they'd finished their coffee and dessert, Laura asked if Craig would like to come back to her place.

"I can't stay all night," Craig said. "I have to get back to my wife."

"I won't keep you all night. Just come to my place and screw me hard," she whispered in his ear as they walked out the door.

Craig gave a low growl and said, "Race you there."

Craig began unbuttoning Laura's blouse in the elevator to her penthouse. He really wanted to do her right there in the elevator, but Laura reminded him there were cameras inside.

Fanning the Flames

She pulled her blouse closed until the elevator doors opened, then pulled him out of the elevator and straight to her front door. As soon as they entered her condo, Craig pulled her blouse open and unhooked her bra. He cupped her breasts, then pulled her down on her couch and began sucking her nipples.

Laura felt herself getting aroused. She remembered how Craig was in bed. He was wild. She liked wild.

"Did you take your little blue pill today?" Laura asked.

"I took it right before dinner. I'm ready to screw you hard, just like you want, baby."

"Let's go to the bedroom," she said. "I'm ready for a little spanking."

Craig groaned. His penis was straining against his khaki pants. Laura reached down and gave his dick a hard squeeze.

Craig yelped. "Hey, not so hard."

"You know you like it," Laura purred. "You know you like it rough too."

"Jesus, I've missed you."

"Let's go."

As they tumbled into Laura's bedroom, Laura wriggled out of her skirt and panties. Craig pulled his pants off as quickly as he could. Craig pushed Laura to her knees and shoved his penis into Laura's mouth and she began sucking hard. He held her head, getting her to stroke him rhythmically.

But he didn't want to cum in her mouth. He wanted to fuck her. Craig pulled Laura up and pushed her down on her bed. He flipped her over and entered her from behind, stroking into her doggy style. He was so close to creaming her.

Since he had taken Viagra, he knew he could hold off on orgasming. He really wanted to enter Laura's anus. She was so tight. Craig groaned his pleasure.

"Where's your lube?" he whispered in her ear.

Laura tried to reach for her bedside drawer, but Craig felt he was about to orgasm. Just thinking about Laura's tight ass, even if he didn't enter her, got him so excited.

Laura didn't mind the doggy style but was less thrilled with anal sex. The fact Craig was still doing her doggy style was just fine.

Craig kept working Laura's breasts, giving them a squeeze, then pinching her nipples.

"Not too hard, baby," she said. "Why don't you play with my clit? I love that."

Craig reached around Laura's legs and began stroking the sweet spot between her labia. Laura moaned. That was going to help her achieve orgasm.

But before she could get there, Craig began to gasp out his orgasm. Laura ended up faking hers. Honestly, she was going to have to use her vibrator tonight after Craig left.

Slightly sweaty, Craig collapsed on the bed panting. "Jesus, I love this. I can't do any of this with my wife. She won't suck my dick. She won't do it doggy. And God knows she won't let me near her ass. She says a good Christian woman should only do it in the missionary position. She lays there like a dead fish."

Craig rolled over to face Laura. "I love that you do what she won't do with me."

Laura just agreed with breathy affirmations. "Oh, yes, Craig. You fill me up. You're just so big. I love it when we have sex."

Most of what she said was just stroking his big ego. He did have a big dick. That part was true. And she did enjoy sex with him when it didn't involve her ass.

Laura laid back in her bed, then poked Craig in the ribs when he got quiet. "Don't fall asleep. You need to go home to your wife. Unless you are going to stay the night."

Craig, sleepy from the sex, declined to stay. "I can't explain an overnight stay to my wife. She thinks I'm at a business dinner tonight. Maybe I can make an excuse for a weekend getaway and come here."

"If you are going to say you are on a weekend getaway, let's go somewhere. Maybe the mountains or the beach."

"It would be cheaper to stay at your place."

"But I'd like you to take me somewhere. I want a getaway, too."

"We'll see," Craig said, as he got dressed to leave.

"Text me tomorrow?" Laura asked.

"Of course."

Fanning the Flames

Laura locked her extra security after Craig left. She reached for another glass of wine before she headed to bed, taking her vibrator out of her dresser drawer. Now she was ready to have her orgasm.

The next morning, Laura stepped out of the shower, toweling off and wrapping her thick black hair in another towel like a turban. She pulled on a plush robe and padded out to the kitchen.

She was ready to make her Cuban coffee in her cafetera pot. She had done it so many times, she could practically do it in her sleep.

First, she ground the coffee beans to slightly coarse grounds. Next, she filled the basket of the cafetera pot, leveling the coffee with her finger. She inhaled its deep rich aroma. She always bought dark roast coffee. She hated the light roast Americans seemed to prefer.

Laura poured filtered water into the lower chamber of the pot and lit her gas stove. She pulled down a large coffee cup and put one tablespoon of raw sugar in the bottom. She liked her Cuban coffee sweet.

She poured just a little bit of the coffee into her cup and used a small whisk to whip up the froth. She then poured the coffee into her cup, stirring it until the foam rose. It was a labor of love she tried to do every morning she was home. She usually had two cups of coffee, but that first cup was the best when the foam was fresh.

Her penthouse had an open floor plan for the kitchen, living room, and dining room. She didn't use the dining room as a dining room. Instead, she used that as her home office. Laura loved looking out of the floor-to-ceiling windows and seeing part of the Buckhead skyline.

Laura booted up her laptop and began messaging several social media influencers on Instagram, hoping she could begin to cement details on coverage.

Elaine Dennis's IG feed was filled with food images, half with desserts and half with entrees from various restaurants. Laura saw she had nearly 40,000 followers, including the names of some local chefs and pastry chefs she recognized.

She'd remind Simon to start following her as well. Then she wondered if Simon even had any social media accounts. She found Seventh Heaven Restaurant Group did, but it didn't seem to be active.

She'd take care of that and remind Kyle she needed to take over that aspect for the restaurants as well.

As Laura sat wrapped in her towel and sipped her coffee, Elaine responded. She said she was interested in what Buon Cibo would offer in terms of entrees, but she also wanted to know what desserts it would offer.

"Because it's an Italian restaurant, it will have traditional Italian desserts like tiramisu, cannoli, gelato, and panna cotta," Laura answered. She hoped that was true. "But not everyone likes those, so there will be some other offerings as well."

"Will they have torte Caprese? That's one of the desserts I love to make," Elaine said.

"I'm sure Buon Cibo will offer a variety of things."

"Do you know who the pastry chef will be?" Elaine asked.

"We don't have a full staff hired just yet, but I'd like to have you be one of the influencers who will help us get the word out. When that decision is made, you would be one of the first to let your followers know."

"Why don't we go ahead and get together for lunch and work out the details," Elaine suggested.

Laura frowned. She hadn't expected to start so soon. She wasn't even dressed yet. In her mind, she thought she'd get everyone down on her calendar in the next two weeks.

"You mean today?" Laura asked, hoping Elaine was busy and she could put off the lunch until later.

"I'm actually free today. Why don't you come over to my house? I love to cook. I can whip up something simple. Do you have any food allergies?"

"None."

"What's your favorite dessert?" Elaine asked.

"I'm from Miami, so that's easy. Key lime pie. But I rarely like the restaurant kind. It's not made with key limes."

"I think you'll like mine. Come over at noon," Elaine said, giving Laura her address in Smyrna, a suburb of Atlanta.

Laura pulled up to a large house off Anderson Drive in Smyrna with an even larger yard that was well landscaped. Laura was a city girl and

Fanning the Flames

didn't even want to think about the lawn care that went into keeping the grass green and the trees and shrubs trimmed. The house looked like something out of a magazine.

She assumed Elaine Dennis was retired, based on some of her Instagram posts. That surprised her. Most of the social media influencers were younger.

Laura walked up to the front door in her burgundy Gucci dress and matching Gucci pumps. She knew the color flattered her. It was another of her power outfits. She also had her new Hermes bag.

Elaine greeted her at the door. Laura was surprised to find a shorter, older woman with blonde hair and a round face. Elaine wore a cream-colored blouse and stylish designer jeans. She wore slip-on flats. Laura was slightly taller than she in her high heels.

Elaine struck Laura as a housewife, not a social media influencer.

But as she stepped into the foyer, Laura could tell the Dennises were wealthy. Not only was the home on the expensive side – Laura had looked up the value of the home – but the interior looked like it came right out of Southern Living magazine.

The living room walls were light gray, with rose quartz accents. The sofa was a darker shade of gray. Cream accent pillows were on the sofa and some chairs.

Elaine showed Laura the first floor and ended in the airy kitchen that put many high-end kitchens to shame. The Wolf double oven and a Viking French door refrigerator, all in stainless steel, caught Laura's eye.

Laura rarely cooked at her home but recognized the expensive appliances in this kitchen. This would have been in Simon's kitchen if he wasn't renting his place.

"I hope you don't mind that we'll eat in here," Elaine said, pointing to place settings at a small booth at the side of the kitchen. It reminded Laura of a booth at a diner.

"My husband and I usually eat breakfast and lunch here. Well, all meals really, unless we are entertaining a big group."

"Do you often entertain big groups?"

"Oh yes. We host several dinners for charities and causes we are passionate about. We host campaign fundraisers for the politicians we support as well. And I usually host a nice luncheon once a year for the Cobb County Republican Women's Club."

"How did you end up a social media influencer?" Laura asked.

"I love to bake, and I was posting all of my cakes and pies on Facebook, initially, but then started posting on Instagram. It just took off from there. My friends think I should go on one of those baking shows. I certainly watch those Food Network shows, but I don't want to compete. That might take the fun out of it," Elaine said as she put two Cuban sandwiches in her panini press and put plantains in a deep fryer.

"How did you know I like Cuban food?" Laura asked, surprised at the lunch being prepared.

"I looked you up," Elaine replied. "When you said you grew up in Miami and liked key lime pie, I suspected you had Cuban roots. But I found a small bio of you and confirmed it. I hope you don't mind."

"No. I love Cuban food. There are only a couple of good Cuban restaurants here in Atlanta."

Elaine plated the sandwiches and scooped the fried plantains on the side of each plate.

"Be careful. These will be very hot. Would you object to some white wine with lunch?"

"That would be lovely."

Elaine had placed water glasses on the table, but then pulled out a Chardonnay from her wine refrigerator and opened it. She filled two wine glasses.

"Please, sit," she told Laura.

Laura sat opposite Elaine in the cozy booth and speared a plantain. She blew on it before she popped it in her mouth.

Elaine had salted the plantains with coarse sea salt and the sweet and salty plantains were good. Laura nodded her head and speared another one.

"These are very good," Laura said. Next, she bit into her sandwich. The tastes reminded her of her grandmother's sandwiches back in their predominantly Cuban neighborhood in Miami.

Once the pair finished eating, Elaine cleared the plates and showed Laura back to the living room, where they sat on the sofa.

With a budget already hammered out with Kyle, Laura pulled out some notes from her handbag and explained what she hoped to

Fanning the Flames

accomplish for Buon Cibo with Elaine's help, and several other select influencers.

"I'm trying to create a buzz for the restaurant ahead of the opening. The restaurant is being designed now and won't be ready for a few months yet. But I've asked Simon Beck to host some menu tastings and chef's tables for just a few of you."

"And what kind of compensation can we expect?" Elaine asked.

"We are willing to pay a flat fee per post for the first six months of the campaign for a total of $3,000 for the entire campaign. If you post more than the $3,000 worth, that's on you. You can invoice me. But I will say, you will be invited to menu tastings regularly, so that's a value-added benefit."

Laura looked up to see Elaine trying to keep her face neutral. Laura continued, "And I'm sure you will gain more followers, as only a select few of you will be given access to some of the content. After that, we can renegotiate. But I expect the restaurant will be open and we'll have other influencers posting for free."

Elaine frowned slightly. She knew what "renegotiating" meant. It meant no more compensation.

"May I give you my answer tomorrow? I'd like to think about it."

That surprised Laura. She thought for sure Elaine, and the others whom she was going to invite to be the elite influencers, would jump at the chance. Laura knew being an elite influencer would also help Elaine, and the others, grow their own following.

"Sure. If I don't hear from you in 24 hours, the offer will be withdrawn," Laura said. "I'm sure you understand I'm reaching out to several others."

"I understand. Now let's have some dessert. I made you a key lime pie. You said it was your favorite, right?"

Laura nodded.

Elaine went to her refrigerator and pulled out a whole pie in a glass pie plate. She took out a silver pie server and cut it. Meringue topping clung to the pie server as Elaine served up a slice to Laura.

Laura's mouth began to water, but she knew she should reserve judgment until she took a bite.

Laura got meringue, the pie, and the graham cracker crust on her fork and popped it in her mouth. Laura nearly wept at the taste. It was as if her late Abuela Rosa had made the pie for her.

Laura swallowed and smiled. "This is very good. Even the crust is delicious. Is it homemade as well?"

"Of course, I do not use store-bought anything. I even squeezed the key limes this morning after our conversation."

"Well, my late grandmother would say 'well done' and so would I. This is delicious. Just like my grandmother used to make."

Elaine smiled broadly. "I'm so glad you like it, and that it is grandmother approved. I have five grandchildren and they like my cakes, too, although they've never asked for a key lime. They are southern born and bred and prefer red velvet. That's what they ask for on their birthdays."

Laura and Elaine finished their desserts and Elaine put plastic wrap over the rest of the pie, insisting Laura take it home.

"But your pie dish," Laura began to protest.

"I'm sure we will run into each other at some point, and you can return it."

Laura was delighted to take the pie home. And she felt sure Elaine would be one of the first influencers on the team.

Chapter 3

Over the next two weeks, Laura met with seven other influencers, taking them out to breakfast or lunch at various restaurants around Buckhead and Midtown. All had immediately said yes to being an influencer for Buon Cibo. Elaine had also agreed. Laura had felt sure she would.

With eight sought-after local influencers, each with a substantial number of followers, Laura felt ready to reach out to Simon for a menu tasting. She was hoping he would agree to host it at his Midtown condo. They could arrange to host four one day and four later in the next week.

Laura was also delighted Craig had sent her flowers after their sexual encounter, along with an orange and yellow Hermes scarf. The gift certainly wasn't diamond earrings, but she could probably return the scarf for the color she wanted instead.

Laura felt grateful Craig remembered to send a gift. Maybe he was just starting small and would work up to diamonds. She sent a quick text thanking him for the scarf.

She added that she hoped they would get together again soon. Laura had an appetite for sex and didn't like to be alone for too long.

Now she just had to call Simon and make sure he would be ready to host two groups of influencers. She wanted it to be perfect. This would set the tone for the entire social media campaign.

Laura decided Elaine, Valerie, Carla Ludwig, and Susie Batson would be in the first group. Maria, Ellen Swift, Eli Tucker, and Angela Yang would be in the next group.

Laura called Simon but got his voicemail. She left a rather long message about having gotten two groups of influencers and asking for dates to host a menu tasting at his condo in Midtown.

Laura, working in her home office, began a small project for Star 1 winery in Napa Valley. She still managed the publicity for the winery and checked on the status of a feature on the property in a California bridal magazine. She'd had photos taken earlier that summer, using models, of brides and grooms, brides and brides, and grooms and grooms.

She messaged Bobby Pearce the progress of that publicity. Laura was glad her interactions with Bobby, the winery manager with whom she'd had an affair, were via email these days. It's not that she didn't care for Bobby Pearce. She cared for him as best she knew how, but she knew she didn't love him. And she didn't want to love him.

She'd also had an affair with the photographer who took the bridal couple photos. She'd enjoyed the sex with the winery manager better.

Kyle had found out about her affair with Bobby and warned her that if she fooled around with anyone at the restaurant, he'd fire her. She smirked. She doubted she would fall for Simon Beck.

She didn't dislike him, but his attitude toward her dampened her enthusiasm for seeking out a relationship with him.

Laura hadn't always disdained men or love. She loved her first boyfriend, Julio — her first love and lover — deeply. Until he raped her to "teach her brother a lesson." Her brother, Ricardo, or Rico to his family and friends, was in a drug gang. The same gang as Julio.

Julio was older than Laura by nearly a decade. He was tender when he took her to bed for her first time. He treated her like a queen. Laura had stars in her eyes and told herself his being in a gang wasn't bad. Just like she lied to herself about her brother's gang activity.

Then Rico crossed the gang, allegedly keeping money he should not have. Laura paid the price. Weeks later both were dead. The police called it gang warfare. She was sure Rico tried to exact revenge for the rape, but also paid with his life.

Fanning the Flames

Laura sometimes had nightmares about Julio's attack. She awoke in a cold sweat, her heart racing, convinced he'd been strangling her.

It was one reason she had the extra security installed on her penthouse's front door. With it, she could sometimes sleep better. Sometimes.

Hours after she finished the work for the winery, Laura stood up, her back stiff. She was hungry and ready for lunch. She had the leftovers from the takeout she got the night before. She opened the white Styrofoam container and sniffed.

She closed the container. She didn't want that.

Maybe she would go down to the gym and work out on the elliptical machine. That would quell her appetite. She'd gained weight on her trip to Napa. The food and wine were good — too good.

After she changed into her workout gear, Laura's cell phone rang.

"Hi Simon."

"What is the meaning of this? This? This menu tasting you want me to host. I don't want to host it!"

"Simon, you said…."

"I never agreed to it. *You* wanted it. It was your idea not mine."

"Simon, you said you would host the menu tasting for the influencers. I have it in my notes."

"Well, your notes are wrong."

Laura was fuming. Her notes were not wrong. She'd all but promised these influencers an exclusive and now Simon was being an ass.

"My notes are not wrong," she argued into the phone. "You promised we could do it at your condo. Obviously, we can't do it at the restaurant. It's not ready."

"Of course it's not ready! We're behind schedule, goddammit!"

Laura could hear frustration in his voice. Was this really the issue? That the restaurant wasn't ready? Laura knew with all construction there could be delays.

"How much is it delayed?"

Simon let out an audible sigh. "A month. Maybe two."

"That's not as bad as it could be. Why don't you and I host a tour of the restaurant for the influencers — even though it is not finished — but a preview of what is to come. Then in a month we can circle back to the menu tasting."

"I do not want people traipsing through the restaurant under construction."

"Why not? I've donned many hard hats and safety glasses to tour condo properties for clients."

"Well, I'm not doing it. It's unsafe and that's final!"

"Then you'd better do the menu tasting. These influencers are champing at the bit to get started on publicity for *your* restaurant."

"You're paying them, aren't you?"

"They sure as hell aren't doing this for free."

"Then you can begin paying them later. I'm not doing a tasting menu anytime soon. I'm trying to get the fucking restaurant built and staff hired."

"Have you begun hiring people? I would think that would come closer to the restaurant opening."

"I've reached out to some chefs and sous chefs I would like to come work for us."

"Poaching from other restaurants here in Atlanta? You might need all the good publicity you can get. Better rethink the tasting menu idea."

Simon was silent for a moment. "OK."

"OK? OK we can do the tasting menu for the influencers at your condo?"

"Where else would we do it?"

Laura sighed with relief. Simon's logic had been circular, but Laura wasn't going to complain. She was going to get what she wanted, and now she'd also pitch a restaurant tour before it opened to the influencers as well.

"Give me some dates so that you can do both events. We'll do one group first, then the other. There will be four influencers at each event."

"You'll be there, right?"

"I said I would. I want to taste your creations too. We'll need wine. Do we want to get some Italian wines you are thinking of carrying at the restaurant or should we have Kyle send some Star 1 wines? I'm sure he'd ship some over."

"He's pressuring me to carry Star 1 wines at all of our restaurants, so I guess we should use those. Maybe he'll give me the friends and family discount," Simon said with snark.

Fanning the Flames

"They are good wines. Almost all reds, though. There are a few whites, but the reds are the best. Let's get some of that Pinot Grigio you had when I was there, as well."

"You are the publicist. You handle it," he said and hung up.

Laura looked at her phone, shocked. Did that asshole just hang up on her after giving her an order?

Laura, still dressed in her workout gear, abandoned the idea of working out. She grabbed her keys and drove to Chick-fil-A for a chicken sandwich and a lemonade. It was her favorite fast food.

She ate it at the restaurant, then drove home.

Laura was in the elevator when her cell phone rang again. This time it was Craig.

"Hey, lover," she purred.

"Can I stay with you? Temporarily, of course."

"What? Why?"

"My wife kicked me out. Says she wants a divorce."

"Did she find out about us?"

"I don't think so."

"Why don't you stay at a hotel or something?"

"Really Laura? I can't come stay with you? Jesus Christ!"

"Hey, it just caught me off guard. I mean we've only just restarted our relationship and now you want to move in?"

"It's temporary. I need to find a corporate apartment or something. But I can't do it today. It's too late in the day try to set up tours of properties."

Laura audibly exhaled. "OK, but just for a few days. I've got work to do."

"I've got work to do, too. I'll be at my office every day."

"When did she kick you out?"

"This morning. Told me not to come back."

"And you waited until now to call me?"

"I sent her flowers and apologized, but she's not having it."

"Sounds like a real shrew."

"She is. Plus, if we live together, we can have sex all the time."

"Temporary. You said temporary."

"Yes, temporary. It's just temporary! Jesus!"

"Do you have clothes?"

"I think most of my clothes are out on the front lawn of my house. I have to run by and get them." Craig tried to cough out a small laugh, but it came out as a slight sob.

Oh God, Laura thought. Is he going to cry? Is she going to have a weepy man at her condo?

"Are you sure you don't want to stay at a hotel? I hear The Mandarin Oriental is nice," she said, referring to a luxury hotel in Buckhead. "You can even get room service. Listen, if you stay there, I'll come stay with you."

Now Craig was angry. "Sounds like you don't want me to stay with you. I thought I could count on you."

"If you need a place to stay — temporarily — you can stay with me, Craig. Don't get excited. I'm just not in the habit of having permanent guests."

"It won't be permanent," he groused. "I'll find a corporate apartment soon. Especially if I'm not wanted."

"Don't be that way. Of course, you are wanted. Why don't you come over after work and we'll go out to dinner?"

"I assume I'm paying."

"Well…"

"OK. I guess I can't complain. Your bed is nice and soft. Especially when you are in it."

Laura rolled her eyes. She knew that was Craig's way of saying he wanted lots of sex with her. She hoped Craig still had money for gifts.

Laura got a quick workout in before Craig showed up at her condo. She'd have to get a temporary parking pass for him. At least it allowed her to put an end date to his stay. He couldn't stay longer than a week or she'd have to pay for a parking space for him. She was not about to pay for that.

The concierge told Laura that Craig was headed up the elevator. She met him on the landing as the elevator door opened. He looked defeated.

"You look awful."

"I feel awful."

"Do you want to go out or should we order in?"

Fanning the Flames

"Can we order in? I don't really feel like going out. You got any booze?"

Laura tried not to show her surprise. "I have vodka, rum and bourbon."

"Rum?"

"For mojitos."

"Can you make those?"

"I can, but I don't have any fresh mint or limes."

"Sounds like a vodka night. What do you have to go with it?"

"Club soda."

"Any Tom Collins mix? I'd love a vodka Collins."

Hands on hips, Laura snapped, "You should have stopped at the liquor store then."

Craig grimaced and grabbed his keys. "Anything else I should get?"

"I'll go with you. We can grab some takeout too."

They went back to the parking garage and went to the liquor store first, then ended up getting Thai takeout.

They returned to Laura's penthouse with Tom Collins mix, a 2-liter bottle of cola and the Thai takeout bags.

Laura mixed a vodka Collins for them both and Craig put the takeout containers on the table. Laura got out some plates after handing Craig his drink. He gulped it down.

"Hey, go easy on that. I want you to be able to get it up tonight."

"Oh, I'll be able to get it up tonight. But let me take my pill."

Craig suddenly frowned. "Fuck. My pills are at my house. Fuck, fuck, fuck."

Now it was Laura's turn to frown. She had a sinking feeling there wasn't going to be any fucking that night.

"Do you really need them?"

"Of course, I need them."

"Can you call your pharmacy? Can you get some extra pills? Explain the situation."

"Pharmacy is closed by now. Laura, it might not happen tonight," he said, fixing another vodka Collins, using more vodka than Collins mix.

"Well shit."

"Cheers," he said, gulping down another drink.

Laura really didn't want to deal with a drunk morose man in her condo. She was regretting letting him stay at all.

Laura hardly slept that night. A drunk Craig was a snoring Craig. Now she saw why his wife kicked him out.

She had had quite a bit to drink as well, but with Craig next to her snoring away, she finally got out her vibrator to satisfy herself. He never even realized what was happening as she groaned out her orgasm. He merely rolled over with his back to her.

Then Laura finally fell asleep. When she got up the next morning, she went immediately to the cafetera and made her Cuban coffee.

Craig stumbled out of the bedroom an hour later.

"Coffee," he commanded, fighting off a hangover. "Lots of coffee."

"I can make regular coffee for you. I've already had my Cuban coffee and I'm not making any more."

"What's Cuban coffee?"

"The best coffee there is. With sugar and milk."

"Yuck. I just want it black."

Laura walked over to her regular coffee maker and made a half a pot of fresh black coffee. She handed Craig a cup and he drank half the cup before handing it back to her. She filled it to the top again.

After Craig and Laura repeated that again, Laura asked if she needed to make another half pot.

"You need to make a whole pot for me. I drink a lot of coffee in the morning, especially when I'm hung over."

Laura nodded. "I'll do that tomorrow. But call your pharmacist today. I want sex tonight."

"Good to know you want some of this," he said, reaching down and giving his crotch a jiggle.

Laura watched with satisfaction as Craig's crotch moved slightly.

Laura walked over to Craig and put her hand on his crotch, rubbing it. "Are you sure need that little blue pill this morning? Can't we give it a go?"

Craig put his coffee cup down on the table. "We can try. Let's go."

He pulled Laura by the wrist back to her bedroom and opened her robe. He cupped her breasts and got on his knees to lick her nipples. At five-foot three-inches, Laura threw her head back and groaned as Craig began to suck her nipples before biting them gently.

Fanning the Flames

Craig reached under Laura's underwear and stuck a finger inside her. Laura gasped. Her whole body began to tingle, and she could feel dampness between her legs. "Craig," she whispered hoarsely. "Don't stop. You are getting me so wet."

Craig stood up and lifted Laura onto the bed, pushing her down, pulling off her underwear, and kneeling to lick her pussy.

Laura groaned with pleasure. Now her hand was on his head. She gently grasped his curly brown hair. This was the Craig she enjoyed. This was the Craig that would get her off.

After a few minutes, Craig raised his body over hers. Laura could feel his penis becoming erect. She reached down and began to stroke his balls and shaft. Craig exhaled loudly.

"God that feels good."

"Do you need me to suck you?"

"That would help. It gets me so excited when you suck my dick."

"Let's get you excited then."

Laura moved and put Craig's dick in her mouth, sucking and rolling her tongue over the tip of his penis. Then she began to suck his balls but returned to his shaft, feeling it get erect. Craig held Laura's head as she worked over him.

"I'm ready," he groaned. "I'm ready for you."

Laura lay on the bed and spread her legs wide. "Come in me, Craig. I need your dick in me."

Craig entered Laura and began stroking inside her. She could feel her orgasm beginning to grow, reaching down, and rubbing her own clit.

"Oh, baby. I'm going to cum. You're going to make me cum," she purred.

"Jesus. Oh, Jesus. Oh! Oh! Oh!" Craig cried out.

Laura could feel him beginning to orgasm and knew her orgasm wasn't far behind. She squeezed her pussy around his shaft as hard as she could, tightening her abdominal muscles, too, and stroked her clit harder.

Craig began to shudder over her body, moaning. She felt him stroking her faster. Soon she was beginning to gasp out her pleasure too.

Chapter 4

Laura awoke with a start hours later, disoriented. What time was it? The light was peeking through her bedroom shades, and she could hear Craig snoring next to her.

Laura sat up with a start and shook Craig hard. "Get up! Get up!"

"What? What?" He asked, not quite awake. "What's the matter?"

"It's late. We slept too late. Get up!"

"Why are you so grouchy?" He asked, rolling over and trying to cuddle with her. "I thought after a good fuck you'd be nicer to me."

Laura punched him in the arm, hard. "Get up. I've got shit to do today and you have shit to do today."

"Hey," Craig said, rubbing his arm. "You don't need to hit me."

"I'll hit you if you make me oversleep."

"I didn't make you oversleep. That was on you. Great sex always puts me right to sleep. Sounds like great sex does the same for you."

Laura got out of bed and pounded into the bathroom, slamming the door. She was irritated already with Craig. He needed to find his own place, and fast.

She turned the shower on and let the water get hot, steaming up the shower walls.

Laura stepped in and let the water wash over her. Reaching for her shower pouf and shower gel, she soaped up her body, running the pouf over her breasts and nipples, enjoying the tingle it provided.

Laura heard the bathroom door open and close.

Fanning the Flames

"Mind if I join you?" Craig asked.

Laura frowned. She did not want him to join her. She needed to shower and get dressed. She was late in starting her work day. She was lucky she didn't have any meetings that morning.

"I'd rather you didn't. You can use the guest bathroom down the hall."

Craig opened the shower door and stepped in. "I don't want to use the shower down the hall. You've got the water just right in here."

"Craig, I said no. I need to shower and get ready."

"Let me help you wash your back," he said, taking the pouf from her hand and running it over her back, starting at her shoulders and moving down to the small of her back.

"I really don't want you in here."

"Let me help you."

"You are not helping. You are getting me horny. And I can see you are getting horny too."

Laura looked down and could see Craig was getting aroused.

"You say that like it's a bad thing. Why don't we both stay in bed today and play hooky from work. We can call in a mental health day. After my wife kicked me out of my own house, I know I need a mental health day."

"Craig, I really need to get some work done."

"No, you don't. Come on, let's play hooky. Just you and me."

Craig began using the pouf on Laura's nipples, then began to run his thumb over her left nipple. His thumbnail scraped over her erect nipple, making her gasp.

"I'll make it worth your while," he whispered into her shoulder.

That caught Laura's attention. She turned to face him in the shower. "How will you make it worth my while?"

Craig turned the water off and stepped out of the shower. "Let's return to bed and discuss the terms."

Laura frowned, seeing Craig was dripping on her floor. She got out and grabbed a towel for herself and threw another one at him. She reached into the linen closet and got another one for her hair. She really should blow it dry, but Craig seemed urgent to return to bed.

"You better make it worth my while. I'm losing money if I don't work."

"How much?"
"What?"
"How much does it cost you to take a day off?"
"I'd have to figure it out."
"Well, why don't you figure it out in bed."
"Is that all you can think about right now? Sex?"
"When it's with a beautiful woman, yes."
Laura smiled at the flattery. "Well, if you pay my lost wages for today, I'll return to bed and call out sick today."
Craig faked a cough. "Me too."

Laura awoke for the third time that day in the late afternoon. She couldn't remember the last time she'd just spent a lazy day making love to a man. Craig had surprised her, not needing to take his little blue pill that day.

He told her it must be because the pressure was off to perform for his soon-to-be ex-wife.

Laura felt ravenous. She had only had coffee that morning and they had skipped lunch.

She poked Craig in the ribs. "Hey, I'm hungry. Take me out to dinner tonight."

Craig pulled a pillow over his head. Laura pulled it off and hit him with it. "Did you hear me? You need to take me out to dinner tonight. And the sooner the better. I'm hungry."

"I'm hungry too. Don't you have anything in the condo?"

"I rarely cook, so there's nothing in the refrigerator."

"You don't cook?"

"If you want a home cooked meal, you need to return to your wife."

"Not going to happen. Can't we order a pizza or something? I don't want to go out."

"I am not ordering a pizza, Craig. You need to take me out."

"See, now that I'm going to have to find a divorce lawyer, and I'm sure my wife has hired some high-priced divorce attorney, I can't be seen in public with you."

Laura's face darkened. "Are you fucking kidding me? I am not going to stay trapped in my condo with you. I think you better find a place to live, now."

Fanning the Flames

"It's not that I don't want to take you out, baby. But I can't be seen with another woman just yet."

"Craig. You need to find another place to live. If you don't want to be seen with me, then we can't be together."

"You're not serious. Let's order some takeout. You go pick it up. I'll pay for it, of course. Please, Laura. I need to stay here just a few days longer. I'll find a place in the next day or two."

"You'd better," she said, angry now. She felt Craig was taking advantage of her and she didn't like men to take advantage of her.

"Listen, call a nice restaurant and order us something nice. I'll pay."

"I'm calling Chops."

"That's fine. I want my steak medium rare."

"Same. I need to pick up some wine, too. Give me your credit card. I want to buy something nice."

"I'd better go with you. You'll end up buying a $300 bottle of wine."

Laura gave Craig an impish smile. "You know me too well."

Laura placed a to-go order at Chops, a high-end steakhouse in Buckhead, and she and Craig stopped at the liquor store before they got to the restaurant. Craig had limited her to buying two bottles of less than $100 red wine.

They waited in the parking circle until the hostess texted Laura that their order was ready. She took the elevator to the restaurant and picked up the order, having paid for it with Craig's credit card.

The meal smelled good as they drove back to her condo. She was hoping the food wouldn't be too cold by the time they ate it.

Laura put both steaks in the oven to get them heated again, but the restaurant had given her instructions to not overcook them. The sides she could heat up in the microwave.

They finally sat down to eat, having already had a half of the bottle of Cabernet Sauvignon. When they finished, Laura said she regretted not ordering some dessert.

"Honey, your dessert is right here," Craig said, pointing to himself.

Laura smirked. "I mean something I could eat."

Craig raised an eyebrow and pointed to his crotch. "Again, right here."

Laura playfully tossed her napkin at him. "You're impossible."

The next morning, Laura got up and got in the shower, leaving Craig still sleeping in her bed.

She was dressed and ready to head to her home office when Craig finally appeared at her bedroom door.

"Why didn't you wake me?"

"I'm not your alarm clock."

"I've got to get into the office today and I'm going to be late," he said, raising his voice.

"Not my problem. And don't get pissy with me," she shot back, her eyes narrowing. "You can set your own alarm on your phone."

"Don't be such a bitch. I just needed you to wake me up. I'm taking a shower. Can you fix me some coffee?"

"Go to Starbucks on your way to your office. I'm out of the kind you like."

Craig shot Laura a look but turned to head to the bathroom and the shower. He returned 20 minutes later dressed and headed for the door.

"Have a nice day, sweetheart," Laura said, unlocking her security system.

"Laura, I can take a hint. I'll find an apartment today if I can."

"That would be best."

"Goodbye, Laura." Craig banged the front door shut as he left.

Laura wasn't quite sure if Craig's goodbye was permanent or not. She didn't let it bother her. She had a job to do and had to make up for the work she missed the day before.

Laura made some calls and returned a couple of calls she'd missed. She also answered some interview questions sent via email for that bridal magazine in California.

By lunchtime, she was hungry and ready to eat. There were a few leftovers from the night before, but she decided to go out. She'd save the leftovers for her dinner that night. If Craig returned to her condo after he got off work, she'd make him take her out.

By seven o'clock that night, she hadn't heard from Craig and decided to text him.

Was he coming back to the condo, or had he found an apartment?

Craig didn't respond.

Fanning the Flames

Laura poured herself a glass of the remaining wine and reheated the dinner from the night before. She sat out on her balcony and watched the setting sun enjoying the meal.

Laura didn't hear from Craig for three days, when he called her to say he needed his stuff out of her condo.

"Did you find a place?"

"Kind of," he said.

"Well, where are you?"

"Back at my house."

"Your house? I thought your wife kicked you out."

"She's had another change of heart. Doesn't want to put the kids through a divorce."

"The kids? Aren't they grown?"

"They are in high school. She wants us to live together, but separately. We can lead our own lives as long as we are discreet about it. So, you and I can still see each other."

Laura frowned. "And what does 'discreet about it' mean?"

"Well, it means we can't be seen at restaurants around Buckhead. But there are lots of good restaurants in Sandy Springs or Cobb County."

"You're crazy. Buckhead has the best restaurants."

"Listen, I'm telling you we can still keep seeing each other."

"You mean you can keep seeing me. It will always be here, at my place."

"Well, yes. I'll always have to come to your place. You certainly can't come to my house."

"I'm not running a hotel," Laura snapped.

"We can go to a hotel sometimes," he said, trying to placate her. "A nice one. We can do that."

"Craig, I can't believe you are back with your wife. You know she's just going to throw you out again."

"No, she won't."

"How can you tell?"

"Because I reminded her, she signed a prenup before we got married. If she divorces me, she won't get the millions she thinks she will."

"Are you worth millions?"

"She thinks so."

"How can you be so sure?"

"Because I handle our finances and she thinks I'm worth more than I am."

"You are devious, Craig. I'm glad I'm not married to you."

"I still have money, Laura. Don't worry. I can still take you to dinner and buy you gifts."

"I should hope so."

"Just not as much. I have to be careful."

Laura didn't like the sound of that. She wanted him to take her out, buy her gifts. She didn't want him to cut back or "be careful."

"Well, I'll leave your things with the concierge at the front desk. You can get them anytime," she said, coolly.

"But I want to see you. I want to come over."

"I think we're done, Craig. I don't want to see you." Laura hung up before he could respond. He tried to call back, but Laura declined to answer. If he was back with his wife but wouldn't take her out to nice places, she was done with him.

Chapter 5

Simon Beck was working hard to get the restaurant designed exactly the way he wanted. He hired the top Atlanta restaurant interior designer, William Paxton. The restaurant would be done in cream, burgundy, and gold tones.

Red hanging lights and gold-tone accents would also be a highlight of Buon Cibo.

Simon knew William wouldn't come cheap, but with Kyle fronting the cost of the new restaurant, Simon didn't think he needed to spare any expense, despite what Kyle sent over as the budget. Once Kyle saw the place, Simon was sure Kyle would approve any overages.

Buon Cibo was being built with a large commercial kitchen with a small chef's table near the kitchen and a large dining area, and – what Atlantans loved – an outdoor patio.

Atlanta diners couldn't resist an outdoor patio, even though the weather for outside dining was limited to mostly spring and fall. Simon planned to have outdoor heaters for winter dining and large fans that could be used in the summer. He wanted his restaurant to have an alfresco option.

Laura visited the restaurant often, watching its progress with a mix of awe and enthusiasm. She had ideas nearly every day for what she could post to Instagram: progress on the dining area, progress on the kitchen, progress on what would be the outside patio. She took photos constantly.

Simon had the idea to install a natural gas-fueled fire pit at one end of the patio. William had convinced Simon it would be used from fall into spring when the evenings were chilly.

Simon loved the idea and forwarded the invoice to Kyle. So far, Simon hadn't heard any complaints from Kyle, so he kept spending money on the restaurant's details. If there were two fixtures and one was more expensive, Simon ordered the more expensive one.

Simon knew he'd end up paying for some of the restaurant construction costs, but Kyle had indicated he'd foot the bill initially.

The patio heaters weren't lined with gold, but they might as well have been since they were top of the line. Simon had the work crew fill two of the heaters with propane and ignite them to see how much warmth they produced, and how close he could space tables around them.

He used a couple of sawhorses and pieces of plywood to imitate actual outside tables, which would be made of metal, not wood. He moved them around the patio but got called to the kitchen to oversee the installation of the overhead hood.

About 15 minutes later, Simon heard shouts from the patio. He walked out to see construction workers trying to put out a fire on one of the sawhorses. Papers left on top of the plywood had caught fire.

Simon quickly went to the kitchen to grab a fire extinguisher but found the stand empty. Where was it?

He ran back to the outside to see the entire propane heater now engulfed in flames and beginning to burn the newly installed canopy to provide partial shade to the patio in the summer.

Flames then began to lick the wood frames of the windows and newly painted decorative shutters.

"Call 911!" he shouted, waving his arms frantically. "Call 911! Clear out! Clear the building!"

Simon gathered the workers at a far end of the sidewalk as he waited anxiously for the fire department to arrive. Just then, he could see Laura's Mercedes-Benz pull into the driveway.

He saw her face register shock and horror as flames began to engulf the front of the restaurant. Simon inwardly groaned. He did not need a hysterical woman on his hands.

Laura pulled into a parking space at the far end of the lot and quickly got out, rushing over to Simon.

Fanning the Flames

"Oh God! What happened?"

"Patio heater caught fire," Simon replied, hoping he could make it look like a faulty heater and his own negligence.

"Why were the heaters on?"

"We wanted to be sure they worked properly. Clearly one did not."

"This is a disaster!" Laura exclaimed.

The pair turned as they heard sirens screaming toward them. Two fire engines and a fire marshal's vehicle pulled in front of the restaurant and firefighters began suppressing the fire.

When the fire was finally extinguished, the fire lieutenant began questioning witnesses. Simon stepped forward to say he saw the fire out on the patio and thought that one of the new patio heaters had malfunctioned. He said he thought it might have been faulty.

"We'll certainly check to see if there was a malfunction," the fire lieutenant said.

"When can we begin to clean up this mess?" Simon asked. "I'm one of the partners of the restaurant and we were building this out to open in a few weeks."

"Well, you won't be able to do any of that right now," the lieutenant said. "It's our investigation now and we can't turn the scene back over to you for at least 24 hours."

"What am I supposed to do until then?" Simon asked.

"Contact your insurance company," he replied.

"This is a disaster," Laura chimed in. "Just a disaster."

"Shut up, Laura. That's not helpful."

Laura's jaw dropped and her eyes narrowed. "Asshole," she muttered loud enough so several of those around her heard her. She turned on her heel, went to her car and left the parking lot.

She called Kyle from the car and got his voicemail. She left a short message that there had been a fire at the new restaurant and there was heavy damage. They weren't going to open on time.

Within 20 minutes, Kyle was calling her back.

"What is it with you and fires at my properties?" he demanded.

"Hello to you, too. And I'm not starting them. I wasn't even there when this one started."

"What happened?"

"Simon said he was testing the new patio heaters and one caught fire."

"So, the damage is minimal?"

"No. It's pretty extensive. It caught the patio windows on fire and looks like it got some of the interior of the restaurant too. If the fire didn't burn anything, the water from the fire hoses made a mess."

"What are you going to do about it?"

"Well, Simon told me to shut up and I left. He is a real asshole, you know that?"

"I'm not paying you to be his friend, Laura. I'm paying you to get publicity for the opening."

"I had a whole plan to use influencers and now that's shot to hell."

"You better start calling the media and get ahead of this."

"Already on it. I'm speaking to a couple of TV stations later this afternoon at the site."

"How long will this delay the opening?"

"I'm not sure just yet. From what I overheard the fire lieutenant say, the scene won't be released for at least 24 hours while they do their investigation. You better check with Simon."

"He's my next call. Keep me updated."

Laura's call was cut off. She was used to Kyle's behavior by now and didn't take offense that he couldn't be bothered with a goodbye.

Laura stood outside the restaurant for a live shot for WXIA, Atlanta's NBC affiliate, and did a pre-taped segment for WSB, Atlanta's ABC affiliate. The CBS and Fox stations just did a brief news item without any input from her.

By the time she finally got home to her condo, she had to deal with an angry voicemail from Simon.

"How dare you call Kyle!" he shouted in the voicemail. "You had no right to call him about the fire. Call me back, Laura. We need to keep our stories straight."

Laura listened to the voicemail twice. She wondered if she could just not call Simon back. She wasn't in the mood to be yelled at that evening. She wanted to have a nice dinner and a couple glasses of wine.

Fanning the Flames

She decided to go back out to the grocery store and get a prepared meal. She didn't like cooking, so a decent prepackaged meal suited her fine.

Laura picked up some barbecue pork, a packaged salad, and some white wine.

After her meal was finished and the bottle of wine nearly empty, she noted two more missed calls and voicemails from Simon.

When Simon called next, she answered.

"Why are you pestering me?" she demanded.

"Why aren't you answering my calls? I left several voicemails saying it was urgent I speak to you."

"I don't see that it was that urgent."

"You don't? A fire has derailed my restaurant opening and that's not urgent?"

"And what, Simon, would you have me do about it at nine o'clock at night?"

Laura could almost feel him seething on the other end of the phone.

"I expect you to return my calls promptly, so I don't have to call you at nine o'clock at night, Laura."

"Well, now you have me. What do you want?" she said testily.

"What are your plans for publicity now? I don't want this to go badly."

"Simon, it's already gone badly. There was a fire and now the restaurant will have to be rebuilt."

"Not entirely. You left before the fire department gave the damage assessment."

"I left because you were being an asshole. Never tell me to shut up again."

"I'm sorry. I should not have snapped at you. I was under some stress this afternoon."

Laura could hear the words, but she doubted they were sincere. "Apology accepted," she said anyway.

"What's the plan now?"

"Well, I did some TV shots for the evening news. Did you see them?"

"No. What did you say?"

"That the fire was a small set back, but that Buon Cibo would still be opening later this year."

"Well done. That's not too far off."

Simon and Laura talked for another hour and a half, trying to come up with some new concepts for the influencers while the restaurant was cleaned up and partially rebuilt. They both estimated the fire had cost them about two months.

"Be at the restaurant site tomorrow around ten o'clock and let's go through the site. Wear casual clothes and shoes you don't mind getting dirty."

"I don't think I have any shoes I want to get dirty."

"Don't you have work boots or something?"

"I have a really nice pair of boots I bought in Napa Valley over the summer, but I don't want them to get dirty either. They are really nice boots."

"Laura, I suggest you go to Walmart and buy a pair of shoes or boots you can get filthy. The restaurant is a dirty, sooty mess."

Laura wrinkled her nose at the thought. "I'll stop by somewhere and get something suitable."

Laura realized she'd finished the bottle of wine during the long phone conversation. She really would have liked another glass as a nightcap, but since she was going to have to stop somewhere for some crummy shoes, she decided to head to bed.

Laura put her dirty dishes in the dishwasher and rinsed out her wine glass.

She checked her security system at her front door, then washed her face, put some luxury night cream on her face and slipped into her soft cream-colored silk sheets.

Laura awoke in a cold sweat. She'd had the same nightmare she'd been having since she was 17. Julio was holding her by the neck and squeezing.

Laura knew she would not get back to sleep that night and got up, checked her front door's security system again, a nervous habit whenever she had that dream, and began to make her Cuban coffee. She took her first cup out onto her penthouse terrace.

The night air was cool but humid. She sat down on a chaise lounge.

Fanning the Flames

She pulled her robe tightly around her, tucked her legs under her and quietly sipped her coffee until the first streaks of daylight began.

She went back into the kitchen and made another cup of coffee, drinking it at the breakfast bar. She pulled out a bowl of cut pineapple, mango, and papaya.

Laura put some of the tropical fruit in a smaller white bowl and cut a large slice of Cuban bread that she slathered with butter and some mango jam she'd bought recently.

She then put on some workout clothes and did a Pilates class she'd recorded on her DVR. She contemplated doing a recorded yoga class, too, but instead went down to the building's gym and got on an elliptical machine and exercised there for 20 minutes.

When Laura had worked up a sweat, she returned to her condo, took a shower, blew dry her hair, and put on what Simon had called "casual clothes." It was a nice pair of jeans and cotton top that if she got dirty, she would be very angry, but it could go to the dry cleaner. Laura rarely ran her washing machine for just a few things.

Laura put on the cowboy boots she'd purchased in Napa Valley. If these got dirty, she'd be angry, but she didn't have any other shoes other than her very expensive sling backs and sandals. She was not going to wear her Jimmy Choos or Guccis to a burnt-out restaurant. And now she didn't have time to stop at Target for some other shoes.

Laura arrived at the restaurant shortly after ten o'clock. She saw Simon's Lexus parked toward the back of the parking lot. She pulled in and parked next to his car under the only shade trees along the side of the lot.

Laura could see some firefighters milling about the front of the restaurant. She wondered what they were doing. One, a young guy, was talking to Simon.

He was cute, Laura thought to herself. She'd be sure to introduce herself.

"Hello," she said, coming up to the group.

"Laura." Simon stated. "This is my publicist," pointing to her. "Catch her up since she couldn't be here on time."

Laura shot daggers at Simon but smiled sweetly at the young firefighter. He was definitely the cutest of the firefighters she saw milling about the restaurant. Most of the firefighters had helmets on inside the restaurant. Those outside did not, and some of them had shaved heads. Laura didn't care for bald men.

"Sorry, traffic in Buckhead."

"You live 10 minutes from here, Laura," Simon said sharply.

Laura stuck her hand out for the young man, who had blond buzz-cut hair and green eyes. "Nice to meet you," she said. As she reached in to shake his hand, she noticed he was taller than she, but not a tall man overall. Maybe five foot eight or nine inches.

"Nice to meet you, ma'am."

Ma'am? Was she a ma'am to him? Was she old enough to be a ma'am? With a sigh, she realized she was likely old enough to be this young man's mother if she'd kept the baby she'd aborted at 17, after the rape.

"And you are?" she prompted.

"Firefighter Cooper, ma'am," he said, extending his hand. Laura took it and felt his strong grip. She felt a little shiver go through her.

"Does Firefighter Cooper have a first name?"

"Troy. It's Troy ma'am," he said, blushing. He took his hand away but could feel a little spark when he'd touched Laura's hand.

Laura reached into her Hermes handbag and withdrew her business card, handing it to Troy. "Here's my card in case you need to reach me. About the fire investigation, of course."

Simon rolled his eyes at the exchange. "Of course. Now if you two love birds are done, let's go through the restaurant and discuss the damage."

Laura found herself blushing and she could see Troy's ears turn pink. She found it adorable. Troy quickly put on his helmet as they went inside.

She followed Simon and Troy into the restaurant. The smell of charred wood and burnt plastic still hung in the air, despite large fans loudly whirring in the corners of the large dining room.

A larger, older man entered the restaurant. "L.T., over here!" Troy called out.

L.T.? Who was that? Laura wondered.

Lt. Dan French, or "Frenchie," to his station, introduced himself. Built like a bulldog, Frenchie was short and stout, without much of a neck.

Fanning the Flames

He had a clipboard in his hand and began explaining where the source of the fire had started. Indeed, it was outside, and likely was one of the patio heaters. His was a no-nonsense demeanor.

"Can we sue the maker of the patio heater?" Laura asked.

"That's for your lawyer to determine, ma'am," Frenchie said.

"Can we file a claim with our insurance company for the damages?" she asked.

"That's up to your insurance adjuster," Frenchie responded.

Simon made a deep frown. He did not want to have to foot the bill for the damages. He wanted someone else to pay.

Laura and Simon stood at the front door of the restaurant as the firefighters and their lieutenant got back in the truck and left.

"Someone was sweet on you," Simon said, smirking at Laura.

Laura hoped she wasn't blushing. "I'm not so sure about that."

"I am. He had those puppy dog eyes when he was looking at you."

"Maybe so. I'd probably be arrested for robbing the cradle. But he was good looking, in that baby-faced kind of way."

"I think you were sweet on him, too."

"I don't think I'd kick him out of bed, if that's what you're asking."

"I was not asking."

"That lieutenant looked a little like a bulldog, with the personality to match," Laura remarked.

"He definitely was not sweet on you."

"Likewise."

"I think we can wrap up this meeting. But Laura, when I say a meeting is at ten o'clock, I mean ten o'clock. I can't have you coming late."

"I was hardly late, Simon."

"So sorry if the meeting interfered with your beauty sleep," he sneered. "I can't have my staff being late."

Laura could feel the anger rise in her. "Simon, I am not your staff," she said through gritted teeth. "I don't appreciate being called your staff or being treated as your staff. I work for Kyle, not you."

"Dammit, just be on time," he barked back.

"What is your problem, Simon?"

Simon let out a long breath. "Shit. The fire might have been my fault."

"What? What are you talking about?"

"I put the patio heaters on to check them, but I walked away. I went to check on the kitchen. Somehow everything out here caught fire," he said, waving his arms at the patio.

"Then it was an accident."

"Is Kyle going to pay for an accident? I'm not so sure," Simon said, pacing back and forth in front on the semi-ruined restaurant.

"Simon, calm down," Laura said, catching his arm and making him stop pacing. "Kyle doesn't want to see his investment go down the drain. Insurance will pay for repairs and Kyle will cover anything extra. But you better come clean about the accident."

Simon looked at Laura with softer eyes. "You think it will help?"

"I think a little humility will go a long way. Don't try to pawn off this as a faulty heater, Simon. It will only cause trouble. Admit that it might have been an accident. Tell him what happened. I think you'll get more sympathy that way."

Simon smiled a small smile. "Thank you. I'm sorry I snapped at you. This just," he said, beginning to pace once again. "I'm just very stressed out."

"I'm here to help you," she replied. "Don't forget that. I'm on your side."

Chapter 6

Laura was surprised, but not disappointed, when she got a call from Troy Cooper. He had a few follow-up questions for her. Could she meet him for coffee? There was a Starbucks not far from the fire station.

Laura parked her Mercedes-Benz in the Starbucks parking lot and entered the coffee shop. She inhaled deeply. She loved the smell of coffee.

The Starbucks was crowded. Laura looked around and spotted Troy, who stood up and waved to catch her attention. Laura motioned she was going to get in line for coffee.

Troy started to move toward her but was hesitant to give up his table in the crowded shop. Laura waved to him to sit back down. She paid for her coffee and sat down next to him at the table.

"I wanted to get your coffee," he said, standing up and pulling her chair out for her. "But we'd never get another table."

Troy sat back down next to her, pulling his chair close to her. Their knees where almost touching.

"It's fine. I used my Starbucks card, so I got points. I'm close to getting another free coffee. You can buy my coffee next time."

Laura saw Troy's eyes brighten. She could tell he was hoping there would be a next time.

"You had some questions? I'm not sure I can answer them for you. Simon Beck is really running the show," she said, trying not to sound bitter. She opened the lid on her coffee and put several packets of sugar in.

"Mr. Beck seems like…"

"A hard ass?" Laura interrupted, stirring her coffee. "Yes, he is."

Troy laughed. He had a nice, easy deep laugh. "I'm not sure I would have called him that."

"Well, I would. And I told you that in confidence," she said, taking a small sip of coffee. "The last thing I need is him hassling me."

She added two more sugar packets, stirred her coffee, and took another sip.

"But you work for him," Troy said, surprised at Laura's comment.

"No, I work for one of the other partners, Kyle Quitman. Simon just bosses me around like I'm his staff. I work for Mr. Quitman. I most certainly do *not* work for Mr. Beck."

"You sound like you don't like what you do."

"No sir, I love what I do. I don't always get along with all of my clients. But I love what I do."

Laura held her coffee in her left hand and put her right hand on Troy's arm. "Do you love what you do? It must be very exciting to be a fireman. And I can tell you are very strong. I guess that comes with the job, huh?"

"I work out a lot. The equipment is heavy, so I have to be able to carry it and load it on my back."

"Have you ever been in any bad fires?" Laura asked, then drank more of her coffee.

"Well, ma'am, all fires are bad," he started to explain. Laura squeezed his arm to stop him.

"Troy, please call me Laura. You make me feel old calling me ma'am."

"Oh, I don't think you're old, ma… Ah, Laura," he stammered.

"Troy, you didn't ask me to coffee as part of the fire investigation, did you?"

Troy blushed and looked down. "No, ma'am. I mean, Laura."

"You just want to hang out sometime?"

He looked up, a smile on his boyish face. "Yeah. I'd like that."

"How about Friday night?"

"Oh." Troy's face fell. "I'm working Friday night."

Fanning the Flames

"Well, why don't you let me know when you aren't working and we can hang out."

"I'm off on Sunday."

"Great. Let's hang out on Sunday."

"You don't mind hanging out with me?" Troy asked. "I mean, you know, I'm younger."

"I don't mind hanging out with someone younger than me."

"Great. I really dig older women."

Laura fought not to frown. "How old do you think I am?"

"Oh, I don't mean your old old. I think you're about ten years older than me."

"Well, how old are you?"

"I'm 25."

Now Laura smiled. "You are exactly right," she lied. "I'm ten years older than you."

In truth, she was over 15 years older than Troy but with Craig out of the picture, she was looking forward to seeing what a younger man could do in bed. She hoped he had staying power.

It wasn't long before Laura found out about Troy's staying power. She invited him out to dinner then invited him back to her place for a nightcap. It was a nightcap that lasted well into the next morning when they made love several times.

Laura was amused that Troy insisted on wearing a condom.

"I can't get pregnant," Laura said.

"Why not?"

"I'm wearing an IUD," she lied. In truth, she assumed that after her illegal abortion in her late teens, she never could get pregnant because she never had gotten pregnant. And she knew that because she's slept with a lot of men, but she'd never admit that to anyone but herself.

"I don't mind. This way we're both safe," Troy responded.

Laura ran her hand over Troy's lean, muscular body, ending at his hip. She made tiny circles on it.

"You are a gorgeous man," she purred.

"You are a very beautiful woman. I enjoy making love to you," he whispered in her ear. He made slight circles with his fingers on her body. "You're hot."

"Careful. You'll get me excited again."

"I can deal with that." Troy grinned at her.

"You can? Can you go again? Honey, you are making me wish I'd been fucking 25-year-olds long before now."

Troy smiled and rolled on top of Laura's body. Laura could feel him stiffening on top of her. Laura moved her hand down to begin stroking Troy's shaft, and then his balls.

Troy groaned his pleasure. "Suck me, baby."

Laura moved lower down his body and took his shaft in her mouth. "Oh, God. Yes!" he said. "You are making me so hard."

Laura continued for a few minutes but was ready to feel Troy inside her. She released him and moved back up to face him. "I'm ready for you. I'm so wet."

Troy reached over on her nightstand and grabbed a foil packet, ripping it open with his teeth. In an adept move that Laura realized Troy did often, he put on his condom and entered her.

Troy rode Laura hard, then mumbled he wanted to do her doggy style. They disengaged and Laura got on her hands and knees on her bed and Troy entered her from behind.

Now it was Laura's turn to groan her pleasure. "Troy, Troy," she panted. Without Laura even asking him to, Troy reached around her and began stroking her clit. She could barely contain her groans.

Laura could feel her orgasm rising. "I'm close, Troy. I'm close."

"Me, too, baby," he murmured. "Me too. Oh, Jesus!"

Laura could hear Troy cry out his orgasm and she rocked back and forth on his penis. Then she felt herself climax.

The pair collapsed back onto her bed, panting and sweaty. Troy carefully peeled off the condom and dropped it over the side of the bed. Laura winced that she'd have three condoms to clean off her floor whenever Troy left. Although she realized, and hoped, that might be much later in the day.

Laura awoke to find Troy getting dressed. "You're leaving?"

"Laura, it's noon. I have to get some sleep before my shift later."

"You can sleep here," she offered.

"Well, I checked your refrigerator and there's nothing to eat. I'm hungry, too."

Fanning the Flames

"I can order some takeout."

"No, I've got to go." He bent down to kiss her. "Will you let me out?"

Laura got up, pulled on her robe, and walked to her front door, punching in the code to undo the locks.

"Why do you have all this security? The place is gated and there's security on the doors to get in the lobby. I imagine there are cameras everywhere too."

"Makes me feel safer."

"Is it up to code?" he asked, eyeing the mechanisms. "In a fire, you might be trapped."

Laura patted Troy on the chest. "Always the fireman, aren't you?"

"I just want you to be safe."

"It's up to code," Laura lied. She had no idea if it was up to code because she'd had a friend of a friend in military security install it for her. She doubted any of it was up to code or legal.

They kissed at the front door and Troy walked to the elevator, pushing the button to lead him to the condo lobby and then to the parking garage.

With Troy gone, Laura realized she was famished, too. She ordered from her favorite Indian restaurant, not far from her condo, and said she'd pick it up in a half-hour. She jumped in the shower, washing her body, but not her hair. That would take too long to dry. Laura would do all that tomorrow.

She arrived at the restaurant just 10 minutes after she said she would pick up the order, which included naan, some samosas, and chicken tikka masala with white rice. Still, she had to wait five minutes to get the order.

She paid for her food, then went back to her condo, poured a glass of white wine, and ate a late lunch. This would probably be her dinner, too. There was enough left over that she could eat more if she got hungry later that night.

Turns out, Laura did get hungry later that night. She opened her laptop and got to work, brainstorming some new ideas for the restaurant, since its opening was now delayed.

Simon, and the contractors who worked on the restaurant, said the fire had set them back at least a couple of months. The contractors wouldn't give an exact time when the restaurant might be ready.

That would mean the restaurant wouldn't open until the Christmas holiday season, a tough time to get buzz about opening a new restaurant. She was hoping she could convince Simon to open the restaurant after the first of the year. Restaurants were slow after the holidays. They could do a soft opening during that time and get the staff fully trained.

Laura's back was stiff. She'd been sitting for too long, hunched over her laptop. She stood up, realizing it was nearly midnight. She warmed up a small portion of the Indian food and poured another glass of white wine. When she was done, she put her dirty dishes in the dishwasher and started it, hearing the faint whoosh of the machine.

Laura checked the security on her front door, turned out the lights and headed toward her bedroom. She was sorry she wouldn't have a 25-year-old body next to hers that night.

Before she turned off her cell phone, she texted Troy something she hoped would make him think of her and get him aroused. It was a heart, the letters UR an eggplant emoji. She smiled as she sent the "love your dick" message.

In the next month, Laura and Troy engaged twice in her favorite kind of sex: public sex. She was glad he was into it, too. They had sex in Stone Mountain Park and Piedmont Park, both of which required a blanket since the temperatures were starting to drop and get cold, especially at night.

Laura asked if they could have sex in Troy's fire station, but Troy gave her an emphatic no for an answer.

"Why not? I'd love to do it where you work."

"I need this job, Laura. If we got caught, I'd be fired."

"We wouldn't get caught. We could do it when a fire call went out."

"No, Laura. Besides, there are security cameras all over inside. We'd still get caught."

At the mention of security cameras, Laura's panties got wet. "That sounds so hot. It's making me hot."

"We are not doing it in my fire station," Troy said, irritated.

"Well, shit. Where else can we go?"

Fanning the Flames

"We can go to my place," he responded.
"Your place? Is it nearby?"
"It's not too far. I live in West Midtown."
"I've never even seen your place. We usually go to my place."
"I know. Let's go to my place. I want to fuck you in my bed."

Laura followed Troy's pickup truck to a loft-style industrial apartment off Huff Road. He led her into a small two-bedroom unit. She looked around to see inexpensive IKEA furniture in the living room and a small kitchen with an island bar and stools around it.

He took her hand and led her back to his bedroom, which was also small. Laura was used to her king-sized bed. Troy's looked like it was a queen bed, with just a beige headboard, which she guessed was also IKEA, and a cheap-looking brown nightstand, with deep grooves and scratches on top. The headboard and nightstand weren't even matching.

Laura could only think of how spartan this apartment was, and how much it looked like a college kid's apartment. She guessed Troy had graduated only a few years ago.

She sat down on the edge of his bed. "Where's your roommate?"
"Working a shift today. We have different shifts."
"He's a fireman too?"
"She is. My roommate is a woman."
"A woman?"
"Yeah. Women can be firefighters too, you know. It's the 21st century," he teased.
"I know women can be firefighters. You just never mentioned your roommate was a woman."
"Well, she is."
"Any hanky panky between you two?" Laura asked, her eyebrow arching.
"Laura, Kara is gay. She's not interested in me in the slightest."
"Oh. Well, I am interested in you," she said, kicking off her shoes.
"You want something to drink? I think I've got some beer."
"I'm not much of a beer drinker. Any liquor?"
"I've got some whiskey."
"Sounds great."
"You want it in a Coke?"
"I'll take it straight up."

Troy went into the kitchen and came back with two glasses. One was just whiskey, and the other was one with Coca-Cola and whiskey.

Laura took a sip and tried not to make a face. This was not her expensive whiskey. She'd have to remember to "gift" Troy a better bottle of whiskey if she ever came over to his place again.

Right now, she didn't think she wanted to return to his place. She realized how much she preferred her place.

Troy drank his whiskey and Coke while Laura nursed her drink.

"You don't like it?" He asked.

"I like it. I just don't want to drink it too fast."

"Well, I'm ready to screw, so drink up."

Laura tipped her glass back and finished her drink, nearly choking as it went down. Troy laughed at her. "Not used to drinking it straight up?"

"I'm very used to drinking whiskey straight up. This isn't as smooth as I usually buy."

"Oh, sorry." He took her glass and put it next to his on the nightstand and crawled over her on the bed. Laura could see his pants straining.

"Hey, get up, I want these off you," she said.

Troy got off the bed. Laura reached for his belt buckle and opened his pants, then pulled down his boxers. She knelt in front of him. His erect penis was now where she wanted it. She put it in her mouth and began sucking. Troy placed his hand on her head as she went down on him.

"Oh, God, Laura. Laura."

She looked up and could see his eyes were closed, a look of bliss on his young face.

Laura stopped the blow job and began sucking his balls. "Oh shit," he said. "Slow down or I'm going to cum all over your face."

Laura stopped. Troy reached into his nightstand and grabbed that familiar foil package. He opened it with his teeth, put on the condom and pulled both of them on the bed. Then he climbed on top of her.

He entered her and began to stroke inside her hard, grunting as he did so. Laura reached down and began to stroke her clit while Troy stroked inside her.

"Ah, ah!" She exclaimed.

"Oh baby, I'm close. I'm close."

Fanning the Flames

"Cum, baby, cum," she told him. "Cum inside me."

"Oh! Oh! Oh!" Troy shouted as he came. Laura let out a high-pitched screech as she orgasmed.

Troy rolled over and pulled Laura close to him. They fell asleep for a few hours and awoke in the middle of the night.

Troy stirred first. "I'm hungry. Are you hungry?"

"I could eat. What do you have? You know my place rarely has food unless we bring it home."

"I know. That's why I suggested my place. I can fix scrambled eggs and bacon. You want breakfast?"

"It's not the morning."

"Well, this is quick and easy. We can eat and then go back to bed."

"You'll be ready to go again after you eat breakfast?"

"Let's find out," he said, grinning at her and swinging his legs over the bed. "Right now, I'm hungry. I worked up an appetite."

He grabbed some pajama bottoms and pulled them up before heading out into the kitchen. Laura didn't have a robe at Troy's apartment. She looked around to see what she could put on.

Laura found a sweatshirt tossed in the corner of the bedroom, pulled it over her head and pulled on her panties.

When she walked out to the kitchen, Troy turned to look at her. "That sweatshirt looks better on you than me," he said, cracking some eggs on the side of a pan and dropping them in.

Laura looked down at the Georgia Tech logo on the front of the shirt. "Did you go to Georgia Tech?"

"I sure did Graduated three years ago."

"And you're a firefighter? Why aren't you an engineer somewhere? I'm sure you could be making lots more money as an engineer."

"Laura, for me, it's not all about the money. I love being a firefighter. It's hard to explain," he said, stirring the eggs as the bacon sizzled in another pan. "There's kind of an adrenaline rush when I head to a fire. I would never get that being an engineer."

"It's all about the rush for you?"

"I guess it is." Troy pulled down two mismatched plates and put half the eggs on the yellow plate and the other half on the green plate. He divided the bacon and put those on the plates too.

Laura and Troy sat at the kitchen island on the bar stools. "Maybe that's why I like the public sex with you," he said with a mouthful.

"It's a rush." He wiped his mouth on a nearby paper napkin and asked, "You want another drink?"

"Yes. I'll take it with Coke this time," she said. She figured the cola would disguise the inexpensive whiskey taste.

Troy pulled down two new glasses and fixed both of their drinks, being generous with the whiskey and using the cola for coloring.

"Whew. This is strong," Laura said.

"Too much for you?"

"No. Not at all."

They finished their breakfast and headed back to bed. As promised, Troy was ready for another round of sex. Laura had felt sure he would be.

Chapter 7

As the restaurant rebuild began in earnest, Simon began to work on the menu for Buon Cibo again.

He asked Laura if she wanted to come over Friday and try a few dishes. Laura wanted to know if he was ready to invite some of the influencers over, but Simon wanted this to be a dry run for the dishes. No influencers, he said.

Laura then asked if she could invite Troy to come.

"Troy? Is that the young buck firefighter? Are you dating him?" Simon asked, surprised.

"Dating might be a stretch," Laura said. She didn't really think of her and Troy dating, so much as sleeping together. Maybe Troy thought they were dating.

"Sure, invite him to come with you. I've got some other people coming as well. About six of us total if Troy comes."

"That's a perfect number for a dinner party. Is it at your place?"

"Of course."

"Great when is it? I need to tell Troy to make sure he's off that evening."

"Saturday night. Cocktails and appetizers will be at six o'clock. Dinner will begin at seven."

"And dessert?"

"Of course. I'm not doing this half-assed, Laura. I will have other chefs there. Ones I respect."

"I understand. I'll be there. I'll let you know if Troy can come too."

Laura had Troy come to her condo late Saturday afternoon, then they took an Uber to Simon's condo. If they were going to be drinking all evening, she didn't want to drive. Plus, with Troy's truck at her place, she was sure she could convince him to spend the night. That would be her real dessert.

The couple arrived a little after six. Atlanta's rush hour traffic coming out of Buckhead and into Midtown was bumper to bumper. Their Uber driver kept drumming his hands on the steering wheel, impatient for traffic to move.

Troy reached over and held Laura's hand in the back seat of the Hyundai Sonata on the drive to Simon's condo. Laura looked down at their entwined hands and frowned. She really didn't want him to think they were a couple.

"I'm nervous about meeting your friends," Troy said.

"They aren't my friends. Simon is a client and I've never met the others who will be there."

"I'm still nervous," he said, whispering in her ear then kissing her neck.

"Don't be," Laura said, waving him off. "I'll be there. You'll sit next to me, and we'll get a great meal out of it. I hope you like Italian."

"I love it. I'll love it better if I'm with you."

The Uber stopped in front of Simon's building and Troy and Laura got out. She asked the driver if he had a card because they'd need a ride home in a few hours. The driver handed her a business card and Laura slipped it into her Hermes handbag.

Simon opened the door to his condo and his eyes widened in surprise. He hadn't remembered how young Troy was. He thought Laura was making a fool of herself and found it embarrassing to introduce Troy as Laura's boyfriend.

Laura caught the surprise on the other guests' faces. Laura frowned as Troy smiled broadly. He was happy to be introduced as Laura's boyfriend and wasn't showing signs of being nervous now.

Laura put on a fake smile as she was introduced to the others in the room. She was most interested in meeting fellow chefs in the room: Tom Halpern, Gideon Stevens, and Zeb Johnston.

Fanning the Flames

Laura made polite conversation with them, Troy by her side.

Simon fixed everyone a Negroni, a traditional Italian gin cocktail. He also had plates of fried Jerusalem artichokes and fried risotto balls with melted mozzarella cheese inside.

Laura sipped the cocktail but watched as Troy took a drink and made a face. Simon saw his reaction and took the glass of Negroni out of his hand. "How about a beer instead? I have some Peroni."

Troy readily shook his head. "That would be great. Sorry. I didn't know there was gin in there. I'm not a fan of gin."

Simon reached into his refrigerator, pulled out the green bottle of beer and opened it on a bottle opener on the side of one of the cabinets. He handed the bottle to Troy. Simon then reached into his freezer for a glass. "Don't you want a glass?"

Troy lifted the bottle toward Simon. "Nope. This is good." He put the bottle to his lips and took a long drink.

Laura frowned again. Didn't Troy realize this was a fancy affair and not a night out with the boys? Of course, he should be drinking his beer from a glass, not like some frat boy at a party at Georgia Tech.

"I'm sure Simon has a cold glass for you though. It would keep your beer colder," Laura said to Troy, trying to prompt him to take the glass.

"No, I'm good. Don't dirty a glass on my account."

Simon smiled at the exchange. Troy was simply too young for Laura no matter how good the sex must be, he thought. And it must be good for Laura to put up with his being a boor and his clueless behavior.

Next, Simon took some eggplant rolls out of his oven. Everyone crowded around as he placed them on a serving platter and grated a little extra parmesan cheese over the tops of the appetizers.

"Be careful. The mozzarella cheese inside is very hot. You'll burn your mouth if you don't let them cool off a little," Simon warned.

"Ow. These are hot," Troy said, popping one into his mouth, then spitting the hot appetizer back onto his cocktail plate.

Laura cringed. It was like Troy was a toddler and didn't listen to instructions.

Laura blew on her eggplant roll before carefully cutting it in half, blew on the forked piece and then ate it. She loved the way the flavors filled her mouth.

"I hope this is one of the appetizers for the restaurant," she told Simon. "These are very good. Troy, you should try one now that they are cool."

"No thanks. I really burned my mouth and tongue. I'll be lucky if I can taste anything at all tonight."

"Shame," Simon replied with sarcasm.

Laura could see Simon was angry with Troy. He was probably angry with her, too, for inviting Troy along this evening. She wished she had just come by herself. Except she wanted sex with Troy later tonight.

Laura just wanted to show Troy off and to show Troy she was a big deal in her professional circles.

A little more than an hour after his guests arrived, Simon had them seated around his dining room table and served up an Italian feast.

He served a molded anchovy dish popular in Venice, a baked gnocchi dish with brown butter, and finally the main dish, saltimbocca. Simon made a show of browning the veal in butter in his kitchen before adding white wine to finish out the sauce. He served a white wine with each dish.

Laura was hoping Simon would do most of these dishes when she invited the influencers over for the tasting menu. Simon was a natural showman.

When he cleared all the plates, Simon served a variety of cheeses before he was ready to pull out a tray of homemade cannoli. He uncorked homemade limoncello he pulled from the freezer.

Finally, Simon served coffee before saying good night to his guests. The meal had lasted four hours.

Laura looked over at Troy, who looked like he was as full as she was. And after two small glasses of limoncello, she was also very glad they were taking an Uber home. It had gone down like spiked lemonade, which ultimately, it was.

Laura was silent on the Uber ride back to her condo. When she and Troy finally arrived, she put in her code for the elevator up to her penthouse.

"Are you mad at me?" Troy asked.

"Troy, I think it's your lack of experience in these social situations that made me angry."

Fanning the Flames

"Lack of experience? What did I do?"

"First, never ever drink beer out of a bottle. Simon even offered you a glass and you refused!"

"But I always drink beer out of a bottle."

"Not at a fancy meal or restaurant you don't."

"Well, next time I won't."

"Then you didn't listen when he told you not to burn your mouth and you did. Then you spit the roll out!"

"I burned my fucking mouth, Laura. What was I supposed to do?"

"You embarrassed me tonight in front of my client and those other chefs. I was hoping I could reach out to them to see if they needed public relations help. Now I'm not sure that I can."

"Well, I'm sorry I wasn't your perfect boyfriend tonight." Troy sighed. "Look, Laura, I'm tired. Let's just go to bed."

Laura huffed into her bedroom, sat on the edge of her bed, and took off her stiletto heels. She began rubbing her feet.

Troy had followed her into the bedroom. "Here let me do that," he said, sitting down on the bed.

Laura swung her legs around and propped her feet into his lap. Troy began massaging her right foot including her arches. Then he began working on her left foot.

Laura moaned with pleasure. "My God, that feels good. Where did you learn to do that?"

Troy also massaged her ankles.

"I love women's feet, especially when they are small, like yours. Kind of turns me on."

Laura took the foot that wasn't being massaged and began to rub Troy's crotch and could feel he was getting aroused.

"Why don't you help me out of this dress?" she asked.

She stood up by the side of the bed and turned her back to Troy, who unzipped her dress slowly. Her emerald green silk dress fell to the bedroom floor.

Troy then unhooked her bra and cupped her ample breasts.

"You really are stacked," Troy said. He gave her nipples a little pull.

"Ah!" Laura exclaimed.

"Laura, I want to fuck you hard," he whispered into her neck.

"Take me, baby," she said.

Troy quickly undressed and tossed Laura on her king bed. He pulled off her thong underwear and shoved his penis inside her, not bothering to put on a condom.

With a quick and rough screw, Laura and Troy climaxed then fell back into bed sweaty, spent, and tired. Both were asleep soon after.

Laura drove to Simon's condo late Sunday afternoon to go over some of the menus she wanted him to fix for the influencers.

She was still irritated with Troy, but after Friday night's rough screw and spending most of Saturday morning in bed with him for more sex, she was less irritated. She smiled when she thought it was a good thing that he was cute and a great lay.

He finally left Saturday to head to his firefighting shift. Laura then texted Simon later that afternoon asking for the Sunday meeting.

Simon greeted her at his condo with "Where's your boy toy? His mother wouldn't let him come out to play with you today?"

"Stop it."

"I didn't realize middle school boys could be out beyond curfew."

"Simon, you're being mean."

"Of course, I'm being mean. He's too young for you, Laura."

"Are you sure you're not just jealous?"

"Jealous? Why would I be jealous of that child?"

"That *man* gives me some of the best sex I've ever had. I bet you can't even get it up anymore."

"Oh, I can get it up, Laura. I'm doing pretty well for myself."

"Simon, let's not argue. I really don't want to talk about my sex life and I sure as hell don't want to hear about your sex life. I want to talk about the restaurant and how to circle back after the fire."

"But I've got to know. What do you talk about after this great sex you are having with him? Current events? The latest issue of Batman comics? Or maybe the latest Iron Man movie?"

"I told you to stop it. I can see why your wife left you. You just won't let it go."

Simon's face fell. "OK. I'll stop. You screw around with whoever you want to. None of my business."

"Now that is something we can agree on."

"What are some of your ideas?"

Fanning the Flames

"I still like the idea of a tasting menu and I think you can use some of the dishes you served Friday night but pare it down to just an appetizer, a main course, and dessert. Then switch to serve some other things with the second group. I want each group to be posting different dishes on social media."

"That's a lot of work to prepare for this. Friday night was a lot of work. I spent most of Thursday and nearly all of Friday to get everything just so. And I have to do it twice?" Simon groused.

"Hey, you are the chef-partner."

Simon suddenly looked weary. "I'm beginning to think this new restaurant is a mistake."

Laura's eyes got wide. "You can't be serious."

"I'm not a young man anymore, Laura. This is turning out to be more work than I expected or wanted, quite frankly."

"Why did you agree to expand then?"

"It's a partnership, remember? Sales were starting to lag in the restaurant group, and my partners drew up financials that showed another restaurant with a different cuisine would lift sales and the bottom line."

"But you didn't have funding for construction, right?"

"Right. That's where Kyle came in. We put out information to some key people who could be investors here in Atlanta. We didn't even put out the information to Black Kat, but he got ahold of it. Or someone else gave it to him."

Simon pulled out a bottle of wine, uncorking it, and poured two glasses, then continued.

"Kyle bought into the partnership and infused the cash for Buon Cibo. But that means creating a whole new menu, hiring, and training new staff, and doing all this social media stuff." Simon waved his hand at "social media stuff."

"But I'm helping you with the social media stuff, as you call it. You aren't doing this by yourself."

"Are you going to cook all the meals for me? Clean up after?"

"We can budget for a small catering company to clean everything up. And if you'll show me how to stir your dishes I'll put on an apron and help."

Simon burst out laughing. "You? I'm not sure you know how to boil water!"

"You don't have to make fun of me," Laura snapped. "My mother was the cook in our family, and she never showed me how. And my grandmother died when I was young. She was the real cook in my family. Even my mother says her dishes don't compare to Abuela Rosa."

"Abuela Rosa?"

"My grandmother's name was Rosa."

"And why did your mother think her dishes didn't compare? I bet they are amazing. Your mother is still alive, isn't she?"

"Alive and well and still living with my father in Miami. I think my mother realized she couldn't get all of the ingredients like my grandmother did in Cuba. The freshest hens, eggs, beef, or pork. Whatever. Seems if it was grown in Cuba, it was better than what we could get in the Cuban grocers in Miami."

"I think that's a universal truth no matter what the cuisine," Simon stated. "I know I'm going to get San Marzano tomatoes imported from Italy, but they won't be nearly as fresh as if they were picked ripe off the vine from a grandmother's garden and cooked in her sauce."

Laura shrugged her shoulders. "Well, I can help — or try to help — you cook some of your dishes. Just show me and tell me what to do."

"You really are willing to help me cook?"

"Yes. I'm willing to try if you need help. I want the tasting menu to go well. We both have a lot riding on it."

"Don't come looking like that," Simon said, pointing to her silk blouse and pants. "And especially not those heels. Your feet will be ruined standing at the stove in under an hour."

"You let me worry about my wardrobe. I have some very comfortable boots I bought in Napa. I wore them when we walked through the fire damage. I can wear those."

"Do you have some old jeans and a T-shirt?"

"I do not."

"What do you wear if you want to paint your condo?"

"I hire people to do that. I don't paint." Laura made a face at Simon.

"I bet your boyfriend has some old jeans and T-shirts. Ask to borrow some from him. Even with an apron, you'll get dirty."

"But I don't want to be dressed like that when the influencers come."

Fanning the Flames

"Bring a nice outfit to change into. Honestly, Laura, it's not that hard."

"What days do you want to do this? We can do it during the week if that will help. Keep your weekends free."

Simon pulled out his cell phone and looked at his calendar app. "I could do it in two weeks on Tuesday. Then maybe the Wednesday of the week after that. In the afternoon, right? Like from one o'clock to three o'clock?"

"I think that's doable. I'll get some invitations worked up and send them out."

"Invitations? This isn't a formal affair."

"I mean digital save the date invitations. I've got to give the influencers time to clear their calendars. But they'd be stupid to miss this opportunity."

"You handle it and be ready to come over early the day of the first event."

"How early is early?"

"I'd like you here by six."

"In the morning?"

"Yes, Laura. In the morning. There will be prep work to do, chopping, stirring, mixing, baking to be ready by one o'clock. You said you'll help, and I will put you to work. So be here on time. That doesn't mean six thirty. It means six o'clock."

"Fine," Laura grumbled.

Chapter 8

Laura set her alarm for 4 a.m. She wanted to shower and make her Cuban coffee before she headed to Simon's condo.

She was irritated she had to wake up early and even more irritated she had to tell Troy he couldn't come over the night before since she had to get up early to help Simon.

"Why do you have to help?" Troy asked. "He's the chef. He knows how to cook."

"He says he needs help prepping all the food and I need this meal to go well so we get some good publicity from the influencers. I even put together a few goody bags for them to take home."

"What's in it?"

"Some gourmet salt, a small wedge of Parmesan cheese, some dried morel mushrooms, a small bag of risotto rice and a recipe for making mushroom risotto I found on the internet."

"Can you give me one and make me the risotto?"

"No. These are for the influencers. Plus, the recipe looks difficult. I'm not even going to try to make it. I'll just order it the next time we go out."

"I'll be off in three days."

"Three days?"

"I'm taking another guy's shift."

"Are you off Saturday?"

"Yes."

Fanning the Flames

"I'll make reservations for Saturday night, then."

Laura always made the reservations. Troy certainly couldn't afford to take her out. She ended up paying for both of them, but always slid her credit card to him so the waiter thought he was paying. She did understand fragile male egos, even if they were attached to burly firefighters.

"OK. Can we go to that steak place again? I liked it there."

"You mean Bones? They have a dress code."

"No. That place where the waiters walk around with the meat on a stick."

"Fogo de Chao."

"That's it. I liked all the steak."

"Sure, I'll make reservations there," she said, inwardly groaning. He would pick an expensive Brazilian steak restaurant in Buckhead. No inexpensive Mexican place for Troy. The sex had better be really good after that heavy meal.

"I don't have to dress up, do I?"

"Nice pants and a collared shirt will do, I think. No jeans, Troy."

"OK. I wish I could come over tonight, though. Even for a little while? I won't stay long."

Laura was tempted. She knew she'd sleep better after great sex. "Not tonight. I'll see you Saturday."

"OK," he replied. Laura could tell by the tone of his voice he was disappointed.

Laura pulled into the parking deck of Simon's condo building. He'd given her the code so she could pull in without buzzing him. She found a parking space in the visitor's area and took the elevator up to his floor.

The sun had not even begun to rise. Laura hated the time change in November. The days were shorter, and daybreak wouldn't happen for at least another hour.

She knocked on Simon's door and was surprised she had to wait for him to come to the door.

When he did open the door, he was in a robe, unshaven, and looked like he'd just woken up.

"What gives? Why are you still in your pajamas?"

"I didn't sleep well last night. Anxious about the event today, I guess. I just woke up when I heard you knocking on the door. I'll get in the shower and meet you in the kitchen in a half hour. There are croissants in a container on the countertop. Help yourself."

"Do you have a microwave? My coffee has gone cold."

"Make a fresh cup. There's a Keurig right there." Simon pointed to the black coffee maker on the countertop.

"But this is my Cuban coffee. I can't make it in a Keurig."

"Suit yourself. Microwave is over the stove."

Simon disappeared down the hall and Laura rummaged through Simon's cabinets, looking for a coffee mug to use to microwave her coffee. She couldn't put her metal travel mug in there.

Once she found the cabinet with coffee mugs, she pulled one down that said, "World's Greatest Dad," poured her coffee into it and warmed up her beverage.

Laura got a plate out and then warmed up a croissant. She sat at Simon's breakfast island and sipped her coffee. She didn't realize he was a father. She wondered how many children he had.

The croissant was buttery and flaky. It was a delicious way to start her morning. Laura stood up and walked out to the balcony. The streetlights still glowed in the Atlanta sky, but sunrise was about an hour away.

For a man who was separated, Simon still had a well-appointed kitchen, she observed. Maybe he couldn't be in a kitchen without his gadgets.

"There you are," Simon said, startling Laura. She nearly dropped the coffee mug. "Sorry. Didn't mean to scare you. Are you ready to get started?"

"I've been ready for the last half hour," Laura said, not hiding her irritation.

Simon's lips went thin. "Very well." He turned on his heel and walked back to the kitchen, grabbing pots, a couple of knives, and roughly put them on the countertop.

"I thought I told you to wear something you could get dirty, Laura." Simon handed her an apron but eyed her nice slacks and silky top.

"I forgot to ask Troy if he had an old shirt. I don't suppose you have one?"

Fanning the Flames

Simon walked back down the hallway and returned with an old T-shirt. He tossed it to her. Laura disappeared into the nearby half bath and came out wearing the shirt. It was a little too big for her.

"Now let's get started," Simon said, holding up a chef's knife. "Chop up these onions and this garlic. These knives are very sharp. Don't cut yourself."

Laura took the knife and tentatively cut into the onion. One half slid across the countertop. She retrieved the half onion and sliced it again. Soon she had a pile of onion chunks and tears were running down her cheeks.

"Glad I wore waterproof mascara today. These onions are strong."

Simon looked over to see the large chunks of onion. He took the knife from Laura and swiftly and expertly minced the pile into much smaller pieces.

"That's how you chop an onion in my kitchen," he said gruffly. "Now do the garlic, and it needs to be minced as well. Minced means small, Laura."

Why was Simon being such an ass? Was it because she called him out because she was on time today and he wasn't prepared?

"Fine," she said, picking up the knife and carefully slicing the garlic. Then she cut the pieces even smaller. "Ah!" she called out.

Simon looked over. "Did you cut yourself? Don't bleed on the food!" he shouted. Simon could see Laura grab her thumb. "Is it bad? Are you cut?"

Laura looked at her thumb, but she'd cut her carefully manicured thumbnail. She really had thought she'd cut her thumb. At first, she was relieved she hadn't cut herself. Then she was mad she'd ruined an expensive manicure.

"Shit. I ruined my thumbnail."

"Be glad you didn't cut yourself. I have no time today to take you to get stitches."

"Do you have a nail file?"

"No. I have nail clippers. You'll probably have to cut that nail off."

Simon once again disappeared down the hall and returned with nail clippers. "Give me your hand."

Laura gave him her left hand and Simon clipped the nail very short.

"Shit, Simon! Not that short! Do you know how long it takes me to grow my nails?"

"You shouldn't have long nails in the kitchen. Cut them all off before you return to help me next time."

"You can't make me cut off all my nails, Simon."

"If you want me to do these menu tastings for your group of influencers you will. I need help in this kitchen," he said, raising his voice.

Laura seethed as she finished with the garlic. She decided she wouldn't come back the next time. Maybe she could hire someone to take her place. She certainly wasn't going to cut off her manicure. She paid a lot for it.

Shortly before noon, Laura was glad she had worn her boots. Standing on her feet the entire morning made her calves ache.

"Are we about done? I need to change into my nice clothes and get the goody bags out of my trunk."

"Goody bags?"

"I got some things to make mushroom risotto and included a recipe. That's what the influencers are getting as gifts."

Simon shrugged. "I guess you are done. Run along." He waved his hand at her.

Laura was stunned. Had Simon just dismissed her? "Well, thank you, Your Highness."

"Laura, you are trying my patience."

"And you are trying mine!" she shouted. "I'm trying to help you and you act as if I'm the hired help."

"Well, aren't you?"

Laura's jaw dropped. "You son of a bitch." She tore her apron off and stormed out of the front door.

Laura fumed as she rode the elevator down to her car. She grabbed her small carryon bag with her change of clothes. She also grabbed another bag with the carefully packed gift bags for the influencers.

She pushed the elevator button and went back up to Simon's floor. With her hands full, she could only kick his front door with her boot. She could smell the pungent garlic from the hallway.

Laura waited in the hallway and Simon finally opened the door.

"I wasn't sure you were coming back," he said flatly.

Fanning the Flames

"If I could have left, I would have, but I still have an event to run," she said, shouldering past Simon and putting both of her bags on the large dining room table.

She pulled out the gift bags and placed them in a neat row. Next, she took her carryon bag and stepped into Simon's small half bath. She locked the door and began changing her clothes into something nicer, a burgundy-colored silk blouse and a black patent leather mini skirt. She also pulled out a pair of black Gucci stiletto heels.

Laura began touching up her makeup, reapplying her smudged eyeliner and mascara, before stepping out of the bathroom.

"Wow," Simon said. "I'm glad you didn't wear this while chopping and mixing. Very distracting."

"I'm glad you think so. Do you need to get ready? They will be here in less than an hour."

"I'll change and then let's celebrate with a small glass of prosecco."

Simon returned a few minutes later in nice dress slacks and a polo shirt with Buon Cibo embroidered on the left breast. He reached into his wine refrigerator and pulled out a bottle of prosecco. He reached up in a cabinet and pulled out two champagne flutes.

Simon expertly popped the cork and poured the pale-yellow bubbling liquid into the glasses. He handed one to Laura and tapped her glass with his.

"To a successful event."

"To a successful event," she repeated.

"We'll finish the bottle after everyone leaves."

"I look forward to everyone leaving, then," Laura said.

Laura was pleased with how the menu tasting had gone. Elaine, Carla, Valerie, and Susie had all arrived within minutes of each other. They oohed and aahed over each dish, taking photos and posting them to Instagram.

Simon made a show of "making" some of the meals, even though they were mostly prepared. But the women wanted so many photos.

His smile became fixed as their smartphone cameras clicked, even though he knew the food was getting cold as each woman tried to get different kinds of photos.

After the appetizers and meal, Simon finally served cannoli and some prosecco for dessert. Two and a half hours later, the women were gone, gift bags in hand.

Laura sat on the bar stool at the breakfast island and rubbed her feet. Simon pulled the remaining bottle of prosecco out of the refrigerator and poured Laura and himself a glass.

"Cheers!" he said.

"Cheers. I think the event went well. I could see them posting a lot of photos and tagging the restaurant in each post. Thank God I set up those accounts a while ago. Just one more group to go."

"All women again next time?"

"No, we have one guy coming in the next group."

"I'll have Kyle ship some more wine. He's pushing me to carry a lot of Star 1 wines in the restaurant, other than the Italian wines I'll carry."

"Have him ship some of the Cabernet Sauvignon reserve. It's really good."

"You've had it?"

"I was out in Napa earlier this year and had some then. Order as much as they have left. You won't be disappointed."

"OK. I'll take your word for it. But if it's crap, you'll have to buy it from me."

"Seriously? If you don't like it, I *will* buy it from you."

"Thanks for your help today. I did appreciate it."

Laura smiled. It was nice to be appreciated, and she was happy Simon acknowledged her hard work.

"I'll be back next week to help again."

"Trim your fingernails please."

"That will not be happening, Simon. I want my nails to be perfect."

"Perfect for what? For chopping and mixing, no."

"For the public relations professional that I am, yes."

Simon raised an eyebrow before seeing Laura to the door.

Chapter 9

Saturday came and Laura was looking forward to her date with Troy. Well, that wasn't exactly true. She was looking forward to the hot sex with Troy after their dinner.

Troy showed up in a dark green polo shirt and black khaki pants. The shirt looked great with his green eyes and blonde hair. She kissed him deeply at her front door.

"You look good enough to eat."

Troy smiled and blushed slightly.

"Do you want a glass of wine or a beer before we go to dinner?"

"Are we going to Uber?" Troy asked.

"We can if you want."

"I don't want either of us to drive home drunk."

"OK. We can call an Uber then. And if we're doing that, I'd like a drink before we go. What can I get you?"

"Beer if you have it."

"I have the beer you said you like. Sweetwater IPA."

"Perfect."

"What are you having? Wine?"

"I'm a wine gal, so yes. I think since we'll be having a lot of red meat tonight, I'll have a Cabernet. I'll probably order that at the restaurant, too."

Laura reached for the wine in her wine rack and pulled out a Star 1 Cabernet. She ordered it every now and again from the winery.

Sometimes Kyle sent her a case for her PR efforts at the winery. She liked it when he sent her the wine. It was expensive to ship.

She pulled the cork out and poured the deep ruby red wine into her glass. Then she turned and clinked her glass against Troy's beer glass.

"I'm glad I convinced you to drink the beer out of a glass."

"Not really convinced me so much as told me not to do it," Troy said, with a frown on his face.

"Well, I just want your beer to be cold," Laura said, catching his frown and trying to lighten the mood. She could feel Troy's mood turning sour. She hoped the sex that night would still be good.

They finished their drinks and Laura ordered an Uber. She frowned when she saw the surge pricing for Saturday night in Buckhead. Now she wished she'd just driven them. But since Troy was a firefighter, he was very conservative about drinking and driving.

They arrived at Fogo de Chao, which was not too far from Laura's condo. She frowned all the way in the Uber until she turned to Troy, then smiled.

They arrived at the restaurant and only had to wait a short while, even though they had a reservation. They were seated at a table for two. Laura ordered a nice Cabernet wine for the two of them. Then waiters began circling them with all kinds of meat on a long thin skewer.

Troy had the waiters stop when they had the filet mignon and prime rib. Laura had lamb and some filet mignon as well. They turned their cardboard circles from red to green when they were ready for more food, then back to red while they were eating.

The bill came to well over $300, as Laura ordered a second bottle of wine. She slid her credit card over to Troy so he could appear to pay the bill.

When the waiter returned with the bill, Troy placed it on the leather bill jacket. All paid, Troy returned Laura's credit card.

Laura ordered an Uber for the ride home. They stood outside the restaurant, waiting for the rideshare. Laura dug deep into her heavier coat.

"The temperature has dropped. It's cold tonight."

"Well, it's almost December," Troy said.

"Do you have plans for Thanksgiving?"

"I'm working that day, so I'll be at the station."

Fanning the Flames

"Will you get a traditional Thanksgiving meal?"

"We always end up with all the fixings. There are some community groups that bring us turkey with all the fixings."

"Lucky you."

"What will you do?"

"I'll probably find some restaurant that serves a Thanksgiving meal."

"You don't cook?"

"Just for me? No."

"Wish I could invite you to the station."

"I'd like that, but I'm sure you can't."

"I can't, Laura. Sorry."

They arrived at Laura's condo and got out. Laura made sure she gave the driver a five-star rating. She knew if she gave the driver a five-star rating, she'd likely get one too.

She and Troy rode the elevator to her penthouse. Laura turned and secured her front door.

She took Troy by the hand and led him to the kitchen. "Want a nightcap?"

"Sure," he said. "But can I have another beer? And can I please just have it in the bottle?"

Laura reached into the refrigerator and pulled out another Sweetwater IPA. But Laura grabbed the Cabernet wine bottle for her.

The pair moved to her living room and sat on the couch. They sipped their drinks before Laura suggested they move to the bedroom.

"Are you ready for the bedroom?"

"Yeah," Troy said, putting his bottle down on an end table. He stood up as Laura did as well. She'd put her wine glass down and moved toward Troy.

She wrapped her arms around him and kissed him.

"You are so gorgeous," she said. She could see Troy blush.

They moved into Laura's bedroom. Troy looked at Laura's king bed. He climbed onto her bed and pulled her onto it with him. Laura flopped on her back willingly.

Troy moved on top of Laura, kissing her, putting his hands under her shirt. Laura moved her hands under Troy's waistband and then his pants.

Laura was reaching for Troy's penis. She wanted to feel him stiffen. She liked to know she was making him get aroused. Laura put her hand on the front of his boxers and began to rub. Troy gave a low murmur from the back of his throat.

"Let's get you out of these," Laura whispered, tugging at his pants and boxers.

Troy kneeled on the bed and pulled off his shirt, this arm muscles bulging. Then he sat on the side of the bed and pulled a familiar foil package out of his pants pocket.

He pulled down his pants and boxers, then kicked them toward the middle of the bedroom.

Laura ran her hand down Troy's lean naked body, stopping at his cock. She wrapped her hand around it and began to stroke it.

"That would feel better if you used your mouth," Troy smiled in the dim light.

Laura smiled back and began to go down on Troy, gently using her teeth when she got to his tip.

Troy gasped. "Oh, Jesus. Sweet Jesus."

Laura kept sucking and stroking rhythmically. But she didn't want him to cum in her mouth. She wanted him to cum inside her.

She stopped going down on Troy and rolled onto her back, undoing her blouse, and wiggling out of her skirt. She spread her legs. "Now me," she said.

Troy began to stroke Laura's clit with his thumb, making small circles on it. Then he used his tongue to lick it before sucking it hard. Now it was Laura's turn to utter a low groan. "Troy, Troy," she panted. "Oh, God, what you do to me!"

"I'm ready," he whispered. He quickly put on a condom and mounted Laura.

He stroked inside her, slowly this time, building the sexual tension between them.

Laura let out a series of gasps and sighs as she felt her orgasm beginning to build.

"Oh, baby. Oh, baby," Troy repeated, his eyes closed tight. "I'm close. I'm so close."

Laura cried out as she climaxed first, but Troy kept stroking inside her before he finally climaxed. He let out a rush of air as he pressed

Fanning the Flames

harder into Laura. "Oh, sweet Jesus," he said. Laura shuddered with a second orgasm.

Troy used his right elbow and rolled off Laura. He peeled off the condom and discarded it in Laura's bedside wastebasket, which she had placed on the floor for just that purpose.

Laura tucked her head on Troy's shoulder and wrapped her arm over his chest. She could feel his heart beating. She could feel her own heartbeat. Her heartbeat began to slow. Soon she heard Troy's soft breathing. She fell asleep curled up next to him.

Troy woke first, getting up and collecting his clothing from the bedroom floor. He sat on the edge of the bed and got dressed.

Laura stirred and sat up, confused as to why Troy was already dressed. She'd expected they'd have a round of morning sex.

"Hey, what gives? Why are you dressed?"

"I've got to go, Laura."

"But I thought we'd have sex again."

"I've got to go," he repeated.

Troy stood up and headed for the front door.

"Hey, but I want more sex."

Laura got up and grabbed her robe, following Troy out of her bedroom. She grabbed him by the arm as he got to the locked front door. "Come back to bed. I'm not done playing with your dick."

Troy shook Laura's grip. "I've got to go. What is it with you and all this security, Laura? I swear this doesn't look up to code." He looked up and down at the door frame.

Laura wasn't sure her system was up to code but lied to Troy easily. "Of course, it is. No contractor would install it if it wasn't."

Troy eyed her suspiciously. "This really could be a death trap if firefighters can't get in during an emergency. Now, let me out."

Laura reluctantly unlocked the system. "When is your next evening off?"

"I need to check the schedule. I'll let you know."

Troy looked the front door up and down as it stood open, then left the condo. Laura pouted as the elevator door closed behind him.

Why hadn't Troy wanted morning sex? He usually was eager to have sex with her the next morning. He usually was eager to have sex with her period.

Laura fixed her Cuban coffee and sat at her small dining table. She had some leftover croissants and heated one in the microwave before she buttered it. She mused over her coffee. What was she going to do with herself this Sunday now that she wasn't going to have delicious sex with Troy?

She didn't really want to work today. She had no qualms about working on the weekends. She often did. But she felt deflated today. Her "boy toy" as Simon had called him, had just left.

Maybe she'd treat herself to some shopping at Neiman Marcus. Or have lunch out. It was now when Laura wished she had some girlfriends that she could do things with.

But Laura was not a girlfriend kind of woman. She was a man's woman. She enjoyed the company of men. Handsome men. Wealthy men. Young men. Men, men, men.

She finished her breakfast and washed out her coffee cup and breakfast plate. She did run her dishwasher now and again, but mostly it was easier to do the few breakfast dishes she used by hand.

Laura stood at her kitchen sink, reminded of her mother Carmela doing all the household dishes by hand. As a girl, she'd sit on the kitchen counter and dry them for her with a pretty kitchen towel embroidered by her grandmother.

Laura took a long shower, letting the warm water run over her naked body. She used her soapy loofah to massage her breasts, circling over her right nipple, then her left. She was beginning to feel aroused. She wished Troy was in the shower with her.

Laura sighed. She'd have to finish her shower and use her vibrator to satisfy her sexual itch. She toweled off and headed back to her bed, laying a new towel on the pillow so it wouldn't get wet. Laura reached for the vibrator in her nightstand drawer.

She fantasized about Troy's body. His hard dick. The way he stroked hard in her when he was about to orgasm. Laura felt her own orgasm begin to build. Soon she felt the tension build and release. She sighed as she felt the satisfying pull of her vagina around the vibrator.

Fanning the Flames

Laura rolled over in her bed and fell back asleep. When she awoke two hours later, it was late morning. By the time she got dressed and headed out, it would be time for lunch.

She thought about texting Troy. Laura shook her head. She'd text him later. She was still kind of mad he'd left her that morning without satisfying her need for sex.

Laura pulled out on Peachtree Road and drove a short distance to Tomo Japanese Restaurant. She was craving sushi. She ordered two rolls, a spicy tuna roll and an eel roll. She also ordered some sushi, including yellowtail and toro, the fatty tuna belly that she found so delicious.

She also ordered the lychee martini to enjoy with her meal. Then she ordered a second one.

When Laura was done, she'd wished she'd ordered an Uber, but she knew it was a short drive home. She suddenly felt tired.

Laura got home and went back to bed, taking a long afternoon nap. When she awoke, she realized she'd missed a text from Troy.

Laura, I've thought a lot about this, and I don't think we should see each other anymore. I hope you understand.

Laura couldn't believe what she was reading. She certainly did not understand.

She tried calling Troy, but it went straight to voicemail.

"Troy, what is going on? I don't want to stop seeing you. Come over. Let's talk about this."

Laura realized she probably sounded desperate, but she was desperate. Why did he want to break up? Didn't he realize men didn't break up with her? She broke up with them.

Laura waited for several hours, but Troy never returned her call. She tried texting him again and calling one more time but got no response.

Now Laura was angry. She was angry with Troy, and she was angry with herself. How could she get him back? She thought she'd send him a nice Tag Heuer watch. Not one that was thousands of dollars. She could find one for under $800. She ordered it and sent it to his fire station.

Lisa R. Schoolcraft

Laura tried texting Troy Monday as well. She finally got a response from him. He said he couldn't keep up with her lifestyle. He was intimidated by her. She was out of his league.

Laura, via text, tried to reason with Troy. But he just texted back that he didn't want to see her anymore.

Troy's watch arrived the next day. He immediately texted Laura that she needed to stop. He was sending back the watch and she was not to call or text him anymore. He didn't want to get a restraining order against her, but he would if she continued to try to contact him.

Laura was livid. A restraining order? What the absolute hell was Troy playing at? The ultimate humiliation came a day later, the day before Thanksgiving, when the concierge phoned Laura to say a watch was at the front desk for her. A young man had dropped it off. He included a note that demanded she not contact him again.

Laura tried not to obsess over Troy, but she kept checking his Instagram account. He posted photos of the Thanksgiving dinner at his fire station. He posted the remains of a building where he had fought a fire. A few days later he posted photos of a puppy.

Laura didn't remember him having a puppy. Whose puppy was that?

He eventually posted a photo of himself with a young woman about his age. He was sitting next to her, smiling, and holding her hand, the puppy in her lap. The Instagram post read: "We are moving in together and got a new puppy. Meet Charlie."

Laura felt as if she'd been punched in the gut. She realized why Troy told her he "hoped she understood." Laura understood she had been dumped for a younger woman.

Chapter 10

Laura showed up the Wednesday after Thanksgiving at Simon Beck's condo in a foul mood. She was there to prepare food for the next set of influencers. Ellen, Eli, Maria, and Angela would be arriving later that afternoon.

"Well, good morning, sunshine," Simon said, sensing Laura's mood.

"Fuck you. I need coffee."

"I'm not sure I can make you Cuban coffee, but I can make you an espresso."

"I'll take it. Make it a double."

Simon went over to his coffee maker and put on the espresso attachment. He made two espressos and poured them into a regular coffee cup.

Laura reached into his refrigerator for milk and asked for sugar. Simon was amused at how much sugar Laura dumped into her coffee before stirring it. Then she added milk.

She took a long drink of the coffee then gave a small smile. "I'm almost human now."

"That's good. The beast that arrived at my door was rather unpleasant. It told me to fuck myself," Simon said in an amused tone.

"I'm just..."

"Just what?"

"It's nothing."

"Boy toy not satisfying you these days?"

"I broke up with Troy."

Simon didn't say anything. He looked at Laura, suspecting that she might not have been the one to break it off. He thought maybe Troy had dumped her instead.

"Well, let's just get through this tasting menu today. You know the drill. Put on your apron and get to chopping and mincing. Mincing means small, Laura."

Simon reached over and grabbed Laura's right hand. Simon looked at her fingernails.

"What did I tell you about your fingernails? They should be cut off."

"Fuck you, Simon. I'm not ruining my manicure for you. I already had to have my thumbnail filled in," she said, showing him her left thumbnail.

"Suit yourself, but you may cut off another one today," he said.

"I'd better not. This fill in was expensive." Laura flexed her hand, looking at her fingernails, then again at her filled in thumbnail.

Laura put on the apron and began chopping onions and garlic. Simon noticed she was handling the knife better than she had the first time. He did hear her sniffling. He wasn't sure if that was from the onions or her state of mind over the loss of her young buck and all that great sex she'd been having.

"Did you have a nice Thanksgiving?" Simon asked, trying to pull Laura out of her mood.

"Absolutely not," she snipped.

"Well, I'm sorry you didn't have a nice holiday. Is your family in Miami?"

"Yes."

"And you didn't go down to visit them?"

"No."

Simon gave up on the small talk. If Laura was going to be grumpy, he'd stop talking to her. The pair continued their work in uncomfortable silence.

"I need you to chop some mushrooms, too," Simon said, breaking the silence.

"Mushrooms?"

"I decided to make mushroom risotto. You're still giving all the ingredients out in the gift bags, right?"

Fanning the Flames

"Yes."

"Well, I thought it would be nice to make it for this group."

"What else is on the menu?" Laura asked.

"Chicken piccata and for dessert some panna cotta with some strawberries."

"What's panna cotta?"

"In Italian, it means 'cooked cream.' It's a little like flan."

"Sounds good."

Simon kissed his fingertips and opened his hand. "It will be *deliziosa*," he said with a flourish. "I made it last night."

"Can I see?"

"It's in the refrigerator. You can see it when I plate it for everyone."

"Can't I see it now?"

Simon wiped his hands on his apron and opened the refrigerator. He pulled out a small ceramic cup and showed Laura the creamy dessert inside. "I have to invert the cup on a plate, drizzle a little chocolate sauce on it and then put the berries on top."

"Oh, OK. It looks good."

"I think you'll like it."

"I have yet to eat anything you've made that I haven't liked."

Simon smiled. "That's high praise, but I'm glad you like everything I've prepared."

"Did you have a nice Thanksgiving?" she asked.

"I spent part of the day with my daughter," Simon replied. "I only made a small meal. It was just the two of us."

"You didn't have anyone else over?"

"No. But if I'd known you didn't go to Miami, I would have invited you over."

"How old is your daughter?"

"She's 20. She's at Georgia Southern University and she was home for the holiday week. She spent most of the time with her mother, but she did come over to spend some of Thanksgiving with me."

"What is her name?"

"Anna."

"She's your only child?"

"We had a son, but he died shortly after he was born."

"I'm sorry," Laura said.

"Are you an only child?" Simon asked.

"No. I had a brother. But he died as well."

"At birth?"

"No. He was killed in gang violence in Miami."

"Oh. I'm so sorry," Simon said, sincerely. "You must miss him."

Laura was suddenly overcome with emotion. She did miss her brother. There were things she wanted to tell him so many times. She was angry with him that he had been in a drug gang and that contributed to his death. But she still did miss him.

"I'm sorry, Laura. I didn't mean to upset you," Simon said, coming over to her and putting an arm around her.

Laura wiped her eyes. "It's fine. He's been gone for more than 20 years. But I do miss him."

"Of course, you do. Here, sit down. Let's have a little prosecco."

Laura sat at the dining room table and Simon brought over two flutes and a bottle of prosecco. He popped the cork and poured out some in each glass.

"What was your brother's name?"

"Ricardo. But everyone called him Rico."

"To Rico and Jacob. May their memories be a blessing," Simon said, clinking his glass against hers.

"Your son was named Jacob?"

"He was. He lived long enough for us to name him."

"My mother never recovered from Rico's death," Laura said quietly.

"I'm not sure my wife has either."

They were quiet again for a moment, sipping their prosecco. Then Simon drained his glass and stood.

"Well, I've still got food to prepare, and you have mushrooms to chop. We'll finish this bottle after everyone leaves."

"Sounds perfect."

They finished preparing the meal. The influencers arrived on time and Laura breathed a sigh of relief. She was sure Simon would not have been pleased with any guest who was late.

She watched in awe as Simon made six chicken piccata dishes and stirred the risotto as the influencers snacked on the appetizers: this time a cheese board and several types of Italian cured meat.

Fanning the Flames

Again, they vied with each other to take pictures of Simon fixing the meal, plating the meal, and photos of the meals before they dug in.

Laura couldn't help but sneak some prosciutto for herself. Simon also served Negroni cocktails to the group but had white wine chilling for the meal.

As Simon served the dessert, he pulled out some limoncello from the freezer and poured small servings. He also started the coffeemaker for some strong Italian coffee with the panna cotta.

As the last guest left, Laura sat back at the dining room table and patted her stomach. "My God, I'm full. I'm going to have to hit the gym to be ready for the holidays."

"I'm glad you liked it."

"What are your plans for Christmas?"

"I'm Jewish. I celebrate Hanukkah. Although this year, it begins on Christmas Eve."

"Sorry. I forgot you told me that."

"Are you going home to Miami for Christmas?"

"Probably not. I expect you and I will be pretty busy with the restaurant. Have you gotten a new finish date?"

"I think we'll be able to do the soft opening in the first weeks of January. I'm kind of hoping I can have a New Year's Eve party for the partners, their wives, and a few guests before we start training the staff. We'll have a soft opening for two weeks while the staff ramps up."

"Can I invite some of the influencers to the soft opening? They can give us some good publicity."

"We'll talk about it. Let's just enjoy this moment. Come," Simon commanded, walking to his balcony, and opening the sliding glass door. "Bring your wine."

"But it's chilly," Laura protested.

Simon reached down and switched on a small portable heater on his balcony. "You sit here," he said, pointing to the chair closest to the heater.

Laura sat down and placed her glass on a small table. Simon sat to her left, putting his glass down too, then returning to the condo and coming out with a new bottle of prosecco.

"Can I interest you in more wine?"

"You most certainly can. But I feel like we should clean up your kitchen."

"I've got someone coming in later tomorrow to do it. I took your advice to hire someone to clean. A woman came yesterday and cleaned my whole condo. She'll come back and clean it again tomorrow. All thanks to Kyle." Simon smiled broadly.

Laura smiled widely back at him. "Smart man. I should have held this at my condo. I would have loved a free cleaning."

"I'm sure you have someone to come to your place."

"I do. But you managed to get a cleaning on Kyle's dime. I'm jealous."

Laura and Simon sipped their drinks in silence, then Laura asked, "Why do you have so much stuff in your kitchen?"

"What do you mean, stuff?"

"Gadgets and things. I don't have nearly so many gadgets."

"You said yourself you don't cook. I do. So, I have gadgets, as you say."

"But I thought you are separated."

"I am. Almost a year now."

"Why so long? Why not just get a divorce already?"

"Laura, it's complicated. We have a daughter together."

Laura shrugged. "Sounds to me like you don't want to get divorced."

"I really don't want to talk about my separation."

"OK. We won't," she said.

"What was your favorite dish?"

"I really liked the mushroom risotto. I wish you'd made that for the first group. They are going to love trying to make it themselves."

"I hope it turns out well for them. Risotto can be tricky," Simon explained.

They killed the bottle of prosecco and Simon asked if he should open another. Laura hesitated. She had planned to drive home, but if she had more wine, she'd have to take an Uber home and leave her car here, meaning another Uber trip to retrieve it.

Laura was also keenly aware that Kyle had told her if she slept with any more of his employees, he'd fire her.

She wasn't necessarily thinking about sleeping with Simon. He was handsome. He had a sort of commanding personality. Sometimes that

Fanning the Flames

commanding personality was off putting. He came across as bossy on more than one occasion.

"Laura? More wine?"

"Sure. I'll have to call an Uber."

"Well, let's see how the evening goes."

Laura looked at Simon, who smiled in return.

Well now, Laura thought. As Simon stepped back into his condo, Laura began debating whether she would sleep with him, if it came to that. Simon wasn't Kyle's employee. He was a partner. He made sure many times to tell her that. She smiled to herself as Simon returned with another bottle of prosecco.

"What are you smiling at?"

"Just enjoying the evening. I'm glad you have this heater."

"The sun should set in about an hour. It's pretty from the balcony."

"Well, you face west, correct?"

"The balcony faces west. The park is right over there," Simon said, pointing toward Piedmont Park. "But my bedroom faces east."

"How do you think the event went this afternoon?" Laura asked.

"You should answer that. You know better than I would."

"I think it went really well," Laura said, pulling out her iPhone and pulling up Instagram. She could see many tags to the restaurant and lots of photos of the food served that afternoon.

"If you think it went well and are pleased, then I am pleased. But I'm glad it's over. This was a lot of work."

"It was a lot of work. But you've done these events before. I know you have because I've been invited to a couple of them at your other restaurants."

"I wasn't doing all the work solo. I had staff to do the prep work. And those were at restaurants that were already open. Not a new one with no staff hired yet."

"Fair point. I'll reach out to the influencers tomorrow to follow up. I'm sure they will all be complementary."

Sunset streaked pink and orange across the sky between the trees down the street. Simon and Laura were quiet as they took in the view.

An hour later, they finished the second bottle of wine and Simon did not ask if he should open a third. He was feeling tipsy, and he could see Laura was feeling the same way when she went back into his condo to use his bathroom. She was swaying slightly. He was thankful she wasn't in her high heels. She might have fallen over.

"I don't think you should drive," Simon said when she returned to the balcony.

"I don't think so either. I should call an Uber."

"Why don't you just stay here tonight," Simon offered. "I have a guest bedroom."

"Oh, I couldn't put you out."

"You aren't putting me out. The sheets are fresh. I changed them after my daughter stayed here last week."

"Well, I'd appreciate it. It saves me the expense of two Uber rides, home and back here to get my car."

Simon led Laura to the guest bedroom. "Would you like a T-shirt to sleep in? I can get you one of mine."

"That would be great."

Simon disappeared into his bedroom and returned with a clean white T-shirt and handed it to Laura. "The guest bathroom is right down the hall," he said pointing. "Good night. Sleep tight."

"Don't let the bedbugs bite," Laura finished, then giggled. She certainly should not have driven home that night.

Simon smiled and closed the guest bedroom door behind him.

Simon settled into bed, thinking about Laura. She was not an unattractive woman. She certainly had sex appeal. He wondered what she looked like naked.

Simon felt himself begin to get aroused. He imagined her voluptuous breasts, her dark nipples, and whether she had any pubic hair. He imagined she didn't. He thought she probably had a Brazilian wax.

Before he knew it, his penis was erect. As he laid in bed, he realized he was going to have to jack off.

With his penis in his hand, he heard his bedroom door open and close. Laura stood at the foot of his bed, darkness surrounding her. Simon couldn't see her face, just a shadowy figure.

"I couldn't sleep," she said. "I was hoping you could help me fall asleep."

She climbed in next to him, entirely naked.

"Dear God."

Fanning the Flames

Simon reached out and stroked Laura's breasts, then he reached down to her pussy and found it smooth as a baby's bottom. He smiled at her in the dark.

Laura ran her hand down Simon's body and found him erect.

"Were you going to start without me?"

"As a matter of fact, I was fantasizing about you, my dear."

"Oh really. Well, lucky you. Fantasy has become reality."

"You aren't wearing the T-shirt I brought you."

"I always sleep naked."

"Then why did you ask for it?"

"I thought it would smell like you."

"And?"

"And it didn't. So, I came here. You smell like you."

"And what do I smell like?"

Laura giggled. "A little like garlic and onion."

Simon laughed as well.

"And you smell lovely," he said, gently sniffing her skin.

Simon rolled over with his arm over Laura. He began to lick her right nipple, which soon became erect. His thumb rolled over her left nipple, and it became erect, too.

Laura was stroking Simon's cock, running her thumb over his penis tip.

Simon gasped as Laura ran her thumbnail over the sensitive spot on his penis tip. Laura could feel a little semen seep out. She hoped he wasn't going to ejaculate prematurely. She wanted him to finish off inside of her.

"See," she whispered in his ear. "You like that I have a thumbnail."

"Yes," Simon whispered back.

Simon's fingers reached down and felt Laura's wet pussy. "Oh, I like this," he whispered.

"I like it too. Put your fingers in me."

"One or two?"

"As many as you can," she said.

Simon put three fingers inside Laura and began to spread them, stretching her walls.

Laura began panting. "Simon. Simon."

"Are you ready for me?"

"Yes, yes. I want you in me."

Simon mounted Laura and entered her, beginning rhythmically stroking into her. He grunted each time he stroked into her.

Laura held onto Simon's arms as he stroked into her. She could feel her orgasm begin to build.

"Oh, Simon. Simon."

"Laura, Laura," Simon repeated. Finally, Simon came, and his final "Laura" came out as one long word.

"Ah! Ah! Ah!" Laura cried out as she climaxed. "Siimmonn."

Laura grasped Simon's back, pulling him closer to her as the walls of her pussy tightened around his penis. She could feel it tighten again and again as she came.

"Oh, God, Laura. Laura," Simon said, as he rolled off Laura, sweaty and satisfied.

Simon smelled Laura's hair as she curled into him. Both Simon and Laura had no trouble sleeping the rest of the night.

Chapter 11

Laura awoke in Simon's arms, a little disoriented. She looked over at him and realized he was not Troy. Then she smiled. Last night was good considering she slept with an older man. Not that Simon was that much older than Laura. She guessed he was in his late 40s since his daughter was 20, and he'd had a son that was probably older than his daughter. She had just turned 41.

Simon stirred next to her and rolled over toward her, slowly waking up. It was then Laura noticed a tattoo of a flame and gridiron on his upper right arm.

"What's this?" she said, circling the tattoo with her finger.

"It's the symbol of San Lorenzo, the patron saint of chefs," he replied, sleep in his voice.

"San Lorenzo?"

"It's new. I got it once I knew we were moving forward with the Italian restaurant."

Laura rubbed her hand over the colorful ink. "I thought Jews didn't believe in tattoos."

Simon smiled. "Well, I might have a Hanukkah bush in my house at the end of Christmas and eat shrimp now and again."

Laura laughed a deep throaty laugh. "You bad boy," she said, tapping him on the chest.

"I like being the bad boy," Simon smiled.

"You know what?"

"What?"

"I like being the bad girl," she whispered.

"I can see that. Are you hungry? I believe I can whip up a decent breakfast."

"I bet you can, but I'd really like to eat you first," Laura purred.

Simon smiled at Laura. "Well. That sounds like a lovely appetizer."

The pair made love again that morning and fell back asleep once they had finished.

A couple of hours later they stirred again. Laura's hair was disheveled, and Simon's salt and pepper hair stood on end.

They laughed easily at how they looked to each other. They got up and Laura returned to the guest bedroom to put on that white T-shirt and her panties, then wandered into Simon's kitchen.

Simon was at the stove, whipping up some eggs in a bowl. "Want some omelets? Sort of a late breakfast now, I guess."

"That sounds good, especially if you are making them."

Simon stood in front of his stove in his boxer shorts and an apron. Laura came around him and wrapped her arms around his waist.

"We have leftover mushrooms, onions, garlic, and some lemon wedges. Will that make a good omelet?"

"Sounds good to me. Everything except the lemon wedges," she said.

"Look in the refrigerator. There might be some peppers or asparagus or something."

Laura opened the fridge and pulled out some vegetables. "I never have much in my kitchen for breakfast, so this is a treat."

Simon made a half turn and kissed Laura on the lips. "Well, I am well stocked."

"I'll say," Laura said, reaching down and giving Simon's crotch a little squeeze.

"Now cut that out, you bad girl."

Laura gave a throaty laugh again. "I think you like a bad girl."

Simon turned to face Laura and with all seriousness, replied, "I do. But don't distract me or our breakfast will burn."

He turned back to his stove and finished the omelets. He reached up and grabbed two white plates and slid the first omelet on one plate, then began the second omelet.

Fanning the Flames

"Please, sit and eat while it's hot. This one will be done soon."

"Can I start the espresso machine?"

"Of course. Do you know how to work it?"

"I think so. And I want some strong coffee."

"You drink that Cuban coffee. I don't like it sweet or with milk. Make mine just black."

Laura made the espresso, filling one cup black for Simon and the second cup she poured several teaspoons of sugar and added a heaping splash of cream that she found in the refrigerator into hers.

Then she finally sat down to her omelet. Simon had also sat down at the table with her.

Simon had shredded some Parmesan cheese over both omelets. They ate in silence at first, sipping their coffee and eating their omelets.

"This is so good," Laura finally said. "Thank you, Simon."

"Well, thank you. It's the little bit of truffle oil on the top," he paused. "I enjoyed last night. I enjoyed you."

"This doesn't have to end, Simon, but I wouldn't advertise it," Laura said, putting her fork down and taking another small sip of coffee. "Kyle made it very clear I was not to sleep with another employee."

Simon raised an eyebrow. "You've slept with one of Kyle's employees?"

Laura was silent before she said, "Well, yes. I have. That's in the past. But he told me he'd fire me if I slept with another one of his employees."

"I'm not his fucking employee, Laura," Simon said, angry. "I'm a partner. A fucking partner! His equal."

"I realize you are a partner. But I think we need to be careful."

Simon thought for a moment. "I think you are right. But I'd like to keep seeing you."

"You will see a lot of me, Simon. Professionally," Laura paused. "And personally, I hope."

"I'd like that."

They clinked their coffee cups together and continued eating their breakfast.

Laura drove toward her condo, still feeling the tingle in her loins. Her time with Simon had been surprisingly satisfying. Yes, he was kind of an ass. But he did know how to work his dick.

Laura got home and opened her messages and checked all the social media accounts for Buon Cibo. She was pleased at how many posts and shares they had. She was also pleased the influencers remembered to use the hashtags for the restaurant. #buoncibo #goodfood #italilanfood #newrestaurant #buckhead #comingsoon

She could follow the shares and likes of the posts. Laura smiled. These were results she could show to Kyle. She took several screenshots, put them in a two-page report with figures of the results, and emailed all of it to Kyle.

Laura had taken some of her own photos of Simon working in the kitchen. She smiled as she looked at them. He looked older than when she looked at her photos. Maybe he was in his early 50s. The salt and pepper hair looked good on him. More pepper than salt, she mused.

Laura laughed at her own small joke. Salt and pepper and Simon being a chef. He wasn't much taller than her and he was lean. Not muscular like Troy, but lean. She started thinking about him and became aroused. Was it too soon to call him and want to see him again?

She didn't have to wonder for long. A text came through.

Still thinking about you. I can still smell your perfume on my sheets.

Thinking about you too. Can we get together tonight? Want to come here?

Do you cook?

No.

Then come here. I'll fix dinner for us.

OK.

7?

See you then.

Laura could barely contain her excitement. She went out for a quick lunch, then got home and began thinking about what she would wear that night. She had some nice cashmere sweaters.

She had a burgundy one and some gray dress slacks. She'd be comfortable in that outfit. And she'd be comfortable out of that outfit.

She packed a small overnight bag: her toothbrush, toothpaste, and a clean pair of underwear. Not that she'd never gone home in the same pair of underwear from the night before. She had done so this morning. But she was happy to pack a clean pair.

Fanning the Flames

Laura contemplated her underthings. She chose a black lace bra and matching thong to wear that night. She packed something more practical for the next morning. She assumed she'd go home the next morning. She hoped she would go home the next morning. She'd make sure she went home the next morning.

Laura tried not to speed down Peachtree that Thursday evening toward Simon's condo. December traffic around Atlanta's luxury malls on Peachtree meant she crawled through each traffic light.

She pulled into the condo's parking garage and took the elevator up to the lobby, then took the elevator five stories up to his place.

Laura found herself feeling damp between her legs. Would he think her rude if she just wanted to fuck him first and eat later?

As she walked down the hallway toward his front door, she could smell something delicious. Her mouth watered. She guessed they'd be eating first and fucking later.

Simon opened his door and wiped his hands on a towel before he led her into his condo.

"You are looking as lovely as ever," he said, smiling, and giving her a quick kiss. "Can I get you a glass of wine? Dinner will be done in about 30 minutes. I'm making a roast."

"I could smell it out in the hallway. It smells delicious."

"I thought a beef roast would be good for a cool evening."

"My mother always made one on Sunday. I'm sure yours will be as good as hers."

"I certainly hope mine lives up to hers," he said. "Come. Sit down. I took your advice and bought a case of that Cabernet Sauvignon reserve from Star 1. You were right. It's just wonderful. I think it will go very well with the roast."

"Then I'm not buying any of it off of you?" Laura smiled.

Simon smiled back. "No. Not a chance."

Simon poured some of the deep ruby liquid into a big-bowled wine glass. He poured another for himself.

Laura started to sip it, but Simon stopped her. "What did I tell you?"

"Swirl, smell, sip?"

"Close enough," he said, smiling. "I'm just teasing you. Go ahead and enjoy your wine."

Laura swirled her wine. She watched Simon as he swirled his wine and tipped his glass to see the wine's "legs." Then he sniffed the wine and took a sip, making a sucking sound and pulling the wine into his mouth. He breathed in as he held the wine in his mouth, then finally swallowed.

"This is a lovely wine. You were correct about it. Thanks for suggesting it."

"I certainly didn't drink it the way you did, but I did know I liked it."

Laura took a gentle sip from her glass, her burgundy lipstick leaving an imprint on the wine glass.

Simon pointed to a plate of smoked gouda and cheddar cheese. There were also thin slices of prosciutto. Laura picked up a toothpick and stabbed some of the cheddar popping it into her mouth. Then she stabbed some of the Italian meat and ate that too.

"Don't spoil your appetite," Simon cautioned.

"Never," Laura smiled over her wine glass, taking another sip.

Simon sat with Laura at the island bar, eating some cheese and meat before putting his wine glass down to check on the roast.

Using two kitchen towels, Simon pulled the roasting pan out of the oven, setting it on top of the stove.

"We'll let that rest for 10 minutes. Bring the bottle of wine over," he commanded.

Laura got off her stool and brought the wine over. Simon took it from her and poured a bit more in the pan. "I used nearly half a bottle on the roast. It should be a very rich au jus."

"Seriously? You used this wine in that roast?"

"Hey, it's free wine. Kyle sent it to the restaurant. I just liberated a few bottles for my home."

Laura gave a throaty laugh. "You are my kind of man, Simon."

He pulled out another pan with roasted root vegetables: parsnips, carrots, turnip, and rutabaga. He took out a microplane and grated fresh parmesan over the vegetables and shook on a bit more oregano.

"Should I bring over the plates?"

"Please."

Laura brought both plates from the table and handed them to Simon. He sliced into the red meat and put the vegetables on both plates.

Fanning the Flames

On the table, Laura lit the two taper candles. She noticed fresh flowers on the table as well. Simon was making an effort, she realized. Simon brought both plates over. "Let me just heat up this bread." He took a loaf of bread and put it in the oven for just a few minutes. Laura sat down, pulling a linen napkin over her lap. Simon came back to the table with the bread and put it in a breadbasket, cutting a few slices with a knife. He then picked up the bottle of wine. He topped off Laura's glass, then his.

"Please," he said, pointing to Laura's plate. "Mangiamo."

"What does that mean?"

"Let's eat."

"That hardly sounds the same as what we say at our house. *Comamos*."

"In any language, let's eat."

The pair made small talk between bites. Simon told Laura about growing up in suburban New York, the son of a grocer. It was how he began his love of food.

"But you don't have a New York accent," Laura said with surprise.

"I moved to Atlanta decades ago. It's home now."

Laura gave a glossed over tale about growing up in Miami. She also gave a brief synopsis of attending Catholic schools. Simon recounted the Hebrew schools he attended.

Before long, they had finished their meal. Laura helped put away the leftovers, putting the vegetables into a glass storage container. Simon sliced some of the meat into thin slices and put them in another container.

"These will make great sandwiches for lunch tomorrow. A little horseradish sauce and some slices of that smoked gouda."

"Stop. You are making me hungry again and I'm full," she said, swatting his arm.

After they'd cleaned up the kitchen and put the dishes in the dishwasher, they went out onto the balcony. Simon turned on the small heater and Laura sat next to it.

"Would you like a blanket for your lap?"

"That might be nice. There's a breeze tonight."

"We won't stay out here long then."

He brought Laura a small lap blanket and laid it across her. Laura tucked it around her legs.

Simon pulled his chair close to hers. They sipped their wine in silence, until Laura asked, "Is there dessert tonight?"

Simon smiled and turned to her. "You are my dessert tonight, my dear. And I'm looking forward to it."

"I think we've been out here long enough," Laura said.

Laura stood up, taking her wine glass and the blanket back inside. Simon turned off the heater and followed her back into the condo.

When they got to the bedroom, Simon turned Laura to face him.

"I guess I should have asked this last night, but you caught me by surprise," he began. "What kind of birth control are we using?"

"Oh, I'm on the pill," she said.

She wasn't exactly lying to Simon. She took birth control pills off and on. But she couldn't remember the last time she had taken a pill. She wasn't even sure her prescription was up to date. She wished she'd told Simon she had an IUD.

She knew she'd told Troy she had an IUD, but the fact was she didn't really think about birth control anymore. She'd never gotten pregnant after her abortion, so she just assumed she couldn't get pregnant again.

"OK. Well, I'm glad that's settled," he said, rubbing his hands down her arms. "Your sweater is so soft." Then he whispered, "But your skin is softer."

When he got to her waist, he began pulling her sweater over her head. Once the sweater was off her body, Simon kissed Laura's left shoulder, then moved lower to kiss the spot above her left breast.

Next, he gently bit through her bra. Laura gasped as she could feel his teeth on her nipple. Simon released his bite and moved to Laura's right shoulder, kissing the top of it, before kissing just above her right breast. He made a little sucking sound as he did so.

He moved down to her bra again and bit through, catching her right nipple. Then he ran his thumb over the fabric.

"This is nice lace."

"It should be. I bought it at a nice shop in New York."

"Does it have underwear to match?"

"It does," she whispered.

"Well, let's see those."

Fanning the Flames

Simon unhooked the side hook of Laura's dress pants and slid the side zipper down with expertise. He pulled down the waistband so that her pants were still around her thighs, but her lacy thong was exposed. Simon grabbed her by her ass, pulling her cheeks apart. Then he slid his finger up under her thong and inserted it in her.

Laura gasped again.

"Shall we play?"

Laura nodded. "But turn out the light."

"No, I want to look into your eyes when I make love to you tonight. I want to see your eyes roll into the back of your head when I take you."

Laura's eyes widened. She liked the thought of Simon making love to her until her eyes rolled back in her head and her toes curled but making love with the lights on always made her feel too vulnerable.

"Please, Simon. Turn off the lights."

"Laura, are you a shy girl?"

"Do you have a dimmer switch? Can we at least dim the lights? It's too bright in here."

"OK, let's dim the lights," he conceded, reaching for the light switch and pushing the dimmer switch down. The bedroom light immediately turned softer. "Better?"

"Much better."

"Now, where were we?"

"I think your finger was in my pussy," Laura whispered in his ear.

"Ah," Simon said. "Would you like me to put my finger back in there?"

"I'd kind of like something else of yours in me."

"And what might that be?"

"Your long, hard cock."

"I might need some help getting it hard."

"And how can I help?"

"I'd like you to suck my dick."

Laura let her own pants slide down her legs and kicked them off, then got on her knees, feeling the plush carpeting under them. She unbuckled Simon's pants and pulled them down.

"Here, let me help." Simon started to remove his pants, nearly toppling over after losing his balance. He then pulled off his boxers. Then he stood back in front of her, his penis beginning to harden.

Laura took his penis in her mouth, beginning to suck it, occasionally taking it deep down her throat.

Simon put his hand on Laura's hair, guiding it as her head moved. Laura suddenly swatted his hand away from her head.

She stopped and looked up at him. "I need to be in control here. Don't do that."

Simon threw both of his hands in the air away from her head. Laura smiled up at him and began to go down on Simon again. Simon groaned and his legs began to buckle.

He threw his arm out and fell to the floor next to the bed.

"Simon!" Laura shouted. "Are you alright?"

"Yes, sorry," he said, embarrassed. "You make me weak in the knees, Laura."

Laura helped Simon to his feet. "Why don't we continue on the bed."

"Good idea."

Laura held onto Simon's arm until he was seated on the bed. She sat down next to him and took his now semi erect penis in her hand and began stroking it and then gave a little squeeze to his balls.

"Are you ready to do me?" she asked.

Laura climbed onto the middle of the king bed and laid back, spreading her legs wide.

"You do like your pussy eaten, don't you?"

"Fair play, Simon. If I'm going to eat your dick, I'd like you to eat my pussy."

Simon laid down next to Laura, beginning to kiss her left breast, sucking, and licking her nipple. Laura knew she wasn't getting her pussy licked this night. Simon was hard again, and he was messing around with her tits.

In her mind, she thought she'd just better get on with the sex.

"Simon, I want you in me," she said. "I need you in me."

Laura was losing her interest and she hoped she wasn't going to have to fake an orgasm tonight. She assumed Simon had a fragile ego and if she didn't make a lot of noise, he would be disappointed.

Simon rolled on top of Laura and jabbed his dick inside her. Laura began to feel her excitement build again. She hoped she could get

Fanning the Flames

toward her orgasm before Simon did. If he came first, she doubted she'd be able to achieve her orgasm.

But Simon was giving her a good strong stroke. Laura concentrated on that stroke, squeezing her pussy walls around his penis.

Simon began to grunt. Laura quickly moved her right hand down and began stroking her clit while Simon stroked inside her.

She could feel her orgasm begin to build. She stroked her clit harder, using her fingernail to scratch across the very sensitive head.

Simon began to orgasm, driving himself deeper inside her. Laura could feel her orgasm as well. She raised her hips. Simon grabbed her ass and arched his back, crying out.

Laura heard herself crying out Simon's name and then let out a yowl. She hoped the condo walls were thick.

Simon collapsed on top of Laura then rolled off her. She could feel some of his semen on her leg and felt it leaking out of her pussy.

She'd need to get up and get a washcloth. She didn't want to sleep in the wet spot in the bed.

"I need a washcloth to clean up," she said.

Simon, panting, pointed toward the bathroom door. Laura got up and ran warm water, finding a washcloth on the towel rod. She wiped herself up, rinsing the washcloth out and replacing it to dry on the rod.

Laura returned to the bed. "Did you bring it with you?" Simon asked. "I could use a wipe down too."

Laura got back up and returned with the washcloth, wiping down Simon's sticky dick. "That's better."

She tossed the washcloth hard toward the bathroom door, hearing it land on the bathroom's tile floor.

Laura curled up next to Simon and fell asleep quickly.

Chapter 12

For all of December, Laura and Simon kept up their affair, working with each other at the restaurant several days a week, then seeing each other almost every night.

Laura was enjoying this relationship. Simon would often cook for Laura, trying out new recipes he was considering at the restaurant. Laura was honest with her comments.

One dish, an octopus dish that used ink in the sauce, left her wanting to order a pizza, and she said so. Simon frowned, then admitted it wasn't his best dish. But he was not about to order a pizza.

He ended up whipping up pasta with mushrooms. Instead of a sauce, he drizzled olive oil over it and added some herbs.

Laura smiled her approval after the first bite. She pointed her fork toward the dish and nodded.

"You need to serve this," she said as soon as she'd swallowed her food.

"What are you doing for Christmas Eve?" he asked.

"Christmas Eve? Didn't you say you are Jewish?"

"Yes. And this year, I told you the first day of Hanukkah falls on Christmas Eve. I'd like to invite you over to celebrate with me."

"But I'm not Jewish."

"You can celebrate your holiday and I'll light the menorah and explain my holiday tradition. I'll have some traditional dishes, too."

"What about Christmas Day?"

Fanning the Flames

"My daughter is coming over for the second night of Hanukkah, so you are on your own there."

"I'll miss your warm body next to mine for the next few days after Christmas. Anna will be staying with me before she visits her mother for the remainder of her holiday break."

"I won't get to see you on Christmas?" Laura frowned. "I was expecting I'd spend the night on Christmas."

"No," Simon replied. "My daughter will be spending a few nights with me. I can still call you at night. We can have some phone sex."

"I'd rather have real sex."

"Do you have a vibrator?"

"Is the pope Catholic?"

Simon smiled at her irreverent joke. "Well, make sure it has some fresh batteries in it when I call."

Now Laura smiled. "Oh, I will."

Laura caught sight of Simon's watch. She noticed it was a Tag Heuer watch, but the watchband looked frayed. It looked like a leather one and was very similar to the one she had bought for Troy. The one Troy had returned to her. She was glad she hadn't tried to return it yet.

"Are we going to exchange gifts on Christmas Eve?"

"Would you like to exchange gifts?"

"I don't want to presume, Simon. I know we aren't exactly dating."

"We aren't?"

"Well, you know. We're sleeping together, yes, but are we dating? If so, we probably shouldn't call it that. Kyle would not be pleased."

"Kyle can go to hell. But I don't like to think we are just fuck buddies, pardon the expression."

"Well, isn't that what we are?"

"That sounds so indelicate. I'd like to think we are more than that."

"Friends with benefits?"

Simon frowned. "I don't think that really describes us either."

"We aren't friends?"

"Of course, we are friends."

"And our friendship includes sexual benefits?"

"Oh, Laura. OK. We are friends with benefits. But that makes it sound so cliche."

"Well, let me ask again. Are friends with benefits exchanging gifts for Hanukkah and Christmas Eve?"

"Yes, Laura," Simon laughed. "Let's exchange gifts."

"I'm not trying to force you to buy me a gift, Simon. But if you plan to give me a gift, I'd like to know. I don't want to be caught off guard."

Simon held Laura's hand. "I would never want to put you in that position. I look forward to what your gift will be to me."

Inwardly, Laura was worried that the watch wouldn't be an appropriate gift. Really, she was just trying to unload it. Maybe she should give Simon something more in keeping with his profession — like a set of knives or something.

Now she was sorry she'd even mentioned exchanging gifts.

Laura arrived at Simon's condo on Christmas Eve in a velvet burgundy wrap dress with her black leather stiletto heels. She wore deep garnet earrings and a garnet ring.

Simon opened his door and gasped. "Laura, I didn't think you could be any more beautiful, and yet you surprise me once again."

He led her into his dining room, where he had the menorah set up on the sideboard table. One white taper was in the middle candle holder, with another white taper that was placed in the right candle holder.

"This candle," Simon said, holding up the middle candle, "is called the shamash. We light one candle each night of Hanukkah with this candle alone. Once we light the candles, we replace the shamash back in its holder. But tomorrow night, we will light the candle to its left first, then the right one next to it, and so on each night."

Simon continued, "We say two blessings each night. But on the first night, we say an extra blessing."

Simon began chanting the blessings. He lit the middle candle, then lit the right candle with the middle candle and replaced it in its holder.

Laura stood silent by his side. The chanting reminded her of being in church, saying blessings to Santa Maria, the Blessed Virgin.

"Hail Mary, full of grace," she whispered, "the Lord is with thee."

"Sorry?" Simon asked.

Laura started. She didn't realize she'd begun to say the prayer out loud.

Fanning the Flames

"I'm sorry. It reminded me of the prayers we say in the Catholic church."

Laura smiled, embarrassed. She quickly changed the subject. "Whatever you are cooking, it smells wonderful."

"You, my dear, are getting a traditional meal tonight. I've roasted a brisket, but I've done it with a homemade barbecue sauce. Then latkes, but I've made them with sweet potatoes. I've made a small kugel. It's sweet. It could be eaten as a dessert, but I've also made sufganiyot."

"Sufganiyot?" Laura asked, pronouncing "soof-gah-nee" slowly.

"They are delicious. They are round, deep-fried yeast dough filled with jam and sprinkled with powdered sugar, so don't get too full. You will want these. If we have any leftovers, we could eat a couple for breakfast with that coffee of yours."

Simon lit more white tapers on the table before he pulled out Laura's chair for her. He then went into the kitchen and returned with two plates full of food.

Simon and Laura enjoyed the meal, drinking some of the Star 1 Cabernet Sauvignon Reserve.

When they were nearly finished, Simon rose from the table and got a small, netted bag, filled with Hanukkah gelt, foil-covered chocolate coins. He placed it in front of Laura.

"What's this for?"

"It's part of Hanukkah tradition. We give each other gelt as gifts."

"Well, I have something for you, as well," Laura said, rising from the table and retrieving a gift-wrapped watch box. She handed it to Simon.

Simon took the box and opened it, surprised at the watch.

Laura could see the look on his face and quickly explained. "Your watchband is frayed. I wanted you to have a new one. I can exchange it if you'd rather just the watchband."

"No, Laura, this is a very thoughtful gift." He took his old watch off and replaced it with Laura's gift. "I think this one might keep better time than my old one."

Simon smiled. "I have something for you, as well."

He pulled a small, gift-wrapped box from his pocket and handed it to Laura.

Laura pulled at the blue ribbon around the silver wrapping. Her eyes widened when she realized it was a jewelry box. She opened it to see a sterling silver cross on a silver chain.

Laura was shocked at the gift. She'd never given Simon any hint that she was religious. She wasn't. She lost her faith after her sexual assault and abortion.

"Turn it over," Simon said.

Laura turned the cross over and saw the word "Rico" etched along the cross. Her eyes filled with tears. Her hands shook as she lifted it out of the box.

"Here, let me put it on you," Simon said. Laura handed the necklace over and turned, allowing him to place it on her neck and closing the clasp.

She put her hand on it. "Thank you," she whispered. "It's beautiful."

"I hope I wasn't being presumptuous by engraving your brother's name on the cross. You indicated you miss him and now you have him close to your heart."

"It is beautiful, Simon. I doubt I'll ever take it off again," she said, putting her right hand across the necklace.

They sat back down at the table. Simon refilled Laura's wine glass, then refilled his.

"I'm glad you like it. Buying jewelry for a woman is a tricky thing."

"Buying jewelry for a man is not easy either," she replied. "I thought about getting you something relating to your kitchen. Maybe I should have."

"Phfff," Simon said, waving his hand dismissively. "I'm glad you didn't. Anything I want or need I can expense for the business. This watch is more personal. Thank you."

Laura smiled her cat-like smile. She was inwardly pleased Simon liked the watch and that she could pawn it off as a thoughtful gift.

"I hope you know I want to show you how much I appreciate your gift."

Simon raised an eyebrow. "Well, I look forward to that. Shall we retire to the couch?"

"Sure. As long as we end up in the bedroom soon."

Fanning the Flames

Laura woke in the night in a cold sweat. Her heart was beating rapidly. She'd had a nightmare about Rico. She had dreamed he was lying in the street, shot, bleeding. His arm was outstretched to her, and he was calling her name.

Simon stirred beside her. "What's the matter?"

"Bad dream. About my brother."

"Oh Laura, I'm sorry. I hope my gift didn't dredge up this bad dream."

Simon pulled Laura closer to him, hugging her in a tight grip. But Laura pulled away from him and got up. "Is there any wine left? I just need a glass to calm my nerves."

"Yes, I can open another bottle."

Simon got up and they both walked out into the living room. Simon uncorked another bottle of the red wine and poured Laura a new glass. He poured himself a glass as well.

Laura stood, naked, in front of the sliding glass doors, looking out into the darkness. Simon had gone back into his bedroom and retrieved his robe. He wrapped a thin blanket around Laura.

They stood in silence quietly drinking their wine.

"I'm ready to go back to bed," Laura said, turning to place her empty wine glass on the coffee table in front of the couch.

Simon placed his half-empty glass next to hers and they walked back into his bedroom.

Laura laid back in the bed, pulling the covers over her. Simon laid down next to her.

Laura reached under the covers and began to stroke Simon's penis.

"Ah, Laura. I'm not sure I can again tonight. I'm not like that young buck boyfriend you had."

"Well, I like it when you play with me."

"That I can do," Simon said, reaching between Laura's legs and playing with her pussy. He ran his finger around her labia before he began stroking her clit. "Nice?"

"Very nice. Stroke inside me, Simon."

Simon placed two fingers inside Laura and began to stroke her rhythmically. Laura groaned. To Simon's surprise and delight, he felt himself get aroused as well.

Laura, with her hand still on Simon's penis, noticed his arousal, too.

"Hey, lover. I think you can again tonight."

"I think you are right."

When they were both sexually sated, Laura leaned back on her pillow and touched her new necklace. Simon noticed.

"Laura, you never talk about going to church. Are you not religious anymore?"

Laura hesitated before she answered. "I lost my faith after my brother died," she said.

She wasn't exactly lying. The death of her brother was just part of the reason she lost her faith. Her sexual assault, Rico's death, and the end of her pregnancy made her feel abandoned by God. She couldn't seem to find her way back to the church. And years later she no longer wanted to return to the church. She felt it was easier to stop believing.

"I will continue to keep you in my prayers, Laura," he said.

Laura put her head near his shoulder and put her hand on his chest. "Thank you," she whispered.

True to his word, Simon called Laura Christmas night and for the next several nights after his daughter had gone to bed.

Laura was surprised at how satisfying the phone sex was with him. He deepened his voice on the phone and almost whispered what he would like to do with her if he were in her bedroom.

But Laura was glad when Simon's daughter Anna left to spend the remaining winter holiday with her mother.

Laura drove south on Peachtree Street toward Simon's condo. She could feel the dampness in her panties as she pulled into his parking garage.

As she rode the elevator to Simon's floor, she could feel her sexual excitement build. She knew she would have convince him to have sex before they had dinner.

When Simon opened his front door, Laura moved in for a deep kiss. "I've missed you, lover," she whispered in his ear. "I can't wait until after dinner."

Simon smiled at her. "Well, it's a good thing I haven't started cooking yet." He took her hand and led her into his bedroom.

Chapter 13

After the New Year, Buon Cibo was nearing completion. Simon spent long hours at the restaurant, too tired to meet with Laura in the evenings.

A few days later, Laura called Simon.

"Have you heard the weather report for Friday?" she asked.

"No, why?"

"The TV station is saying there is a big snowstorm coming."

"So?"

"So, can I come stay with you? The mayor is telling people to be off the streets by Friday afternoon and not to leave their homes."

"Why do you need to shelter at my place? I've been to your penthouse, that one time, Laura. It's lovely."

"Because three years ago in that big storm – the one that shut down the city and people got trapped in their cars on the highway – I was stuck in my condo for a week without much food."

"Without food?"

"I managed to get some takeout and made it last for the week."

"Can't you go to the grocery store right now? Hang up with me and go get some groceries," Simon said, exasperated.

"But I like it when you cook for me. If I'm going to be stuck inside for a week, I'd like it to be with you. If you're going to be stuck in our homes, wouldn't you like to be stuck with me?"

"We are not going to be stuck inside for a week."

"I was in Snow Jam! I was almost out of milk for my coffee."
"No milk! *Quelle horreur!*"
"Stop making fun of me. It was awful."
"How did you survive?"
"I asked the neighbors if they had any milk for my coffee."
"Did that work?"
"Yes."
"Laura, then you are perfectly capable of staying in your condo. You don't need to stay with me."
Laura pouted her displeasure. "Well, fine!" She then hung up on Simon.

Unhappily, Laura prepared to stayed home alone that weekend. She went to the grocery store, which was a madhouse. Most of the shelves were empty of milk and bread. Even her plan to buy rotisserie chickens was thwarted. There were none.

She managed to buy several pints of half and half and bought two boxes of dry pasta. Contrary to popular belief, she could boil water. She hoped her meager purchases would be enough if she had to stay in her condo for at least a week.

While she paced her condo looking out the floor to ceiling windows at the gray sky, she decided to email several influencers, trying to build excitement about the upcoming restaurant opening. She sent out invitations to the soft opening and grand opening. She hoped the predicted snow storm would not delay the restaurant further.

Turns out, the snowstorm was not as bad as everyone expected. There was light freezing rain and fog that Friday night and into Saturday. The weather barely made it above freezing, leaving the roads slick.

Then the temperature rose above freezing and Atlantans hit the roads once more.

With the snowstorm creating nothing more than an irritation for Simon, he got to the restaurant to oversee the training of his kitchen staff. He was not taking the weather as an excuse for not showing up for work.

He fired several staff who were no shows. Simon trained his three new managers, who then oversaw the training of the waitstaff. Every day became controlled chaos.

Fanning the Flames

Laura felt her sexual tension building. He'd rebuffed her attempts to stay with him at his place, but she kept calling to see if she could see him in the evenings.

She wanted Simon, but he kept making excuses as to why she couldn't come over even after the storm. She invited him to her place, but he said he needed to get up early to return to the restaurant.

Laura found herself becoming jealous of Buon Cibo. Her anger came to a head one afternoon as they both worked at the restaurant. She cornered him in the small office at Buon Cibo.

"Why can't I come over tonight? I miss you. I miss your dick."

"Laura, please. Not now. I'm up to my eyeballs in work here and all you can think about is your pussy."

"That's because your dick has been nowhere near my pussy for almost three weeks!"

"You know I've been here! It's not like I've been seeing anyone else!"

"But you haven't even been seeing me!" she shouted.

"Keep your voice down. You sound like a shrew. You sound like my wife."

"Well, I can see why your wife kicked you out. She probably got tired of you ignoring her."

"Ignoring you? I have a job to do! I need to open this restaurant!"

"You act like no one has ever opened a restaurant before! Why do you have to do everything? Why can't you delegate?"

"Delegate? Kyle Quitman expects me to do all the work. He's certainly not here sullying his hands. You don't see him helping me in any way."

"Oh please. You have contractors, sous chefs. You have help."

"I don't need this shit from you," Simon said, throwing his hands up in despair. "You are my employee, and I won't have you speaking to me like this. I demand your respect!"

"Respect! Right now, I don't even like you!" she shouted back.

Laura stormed out of the restaurant and got into her car, returning to her penthouse. She stormed about her condo, growing angrier and angrier.

She reached for a glass of Star 1 Cabernet. She raged at Simon. She raged at his attitude toward her.

After several glasses of wine, she finally texted Simon. She told him she wasn't going to put up with his behavior anymore. She'd like to collect her belongings from his condo. She wanted to end their relationship.

Fine, was his response. Simon said Laura could pick up her things the next evening. He'd meet her at his place at ten o'clock at night.

Laura fumed as she drove to Simon's condo. She was sure he was meeting her this late to spite her. She was going to give him a big piece of her mind when she got there.

She was just sorry she'd still have to work with him on the restaurant's opening. Well, she could do it. She'd be professional, but frosty toward him. Simon deserved it, she reasoned.

When Laura got to Simon's front door, she found her things piled in front of it. On top of the pile was the Tag Heuer watch she had given him as a present.

But it was just the watch, not the box it had come in. Once again, the watch was returned to her. Without the box, she couldn't return it or regift it.

"Simon!" she banged on the front door. "You son of a bitch!"

Fine, she thought. Two could play this game. Laura took the necklace from her neck – the one Simon had given her – and dropped it at the door as she collected her things.

She stormed back to her car, trying not to drop her expensive makeup, makeup brushes, hairbrush, and clothing. She cursed Simon that he didn't have the decency to put her stuff in a bag at least.

Good riddance, she thought as she opened the trunk and dropped her things in. She pulled out of the parking garage and knew she'd never be back.

Chapter 14

Laura and Simon now worked in silence at the restaurant, but she made sure she spent less time at Buon Cibo.

She worked from her penthouse, making last-minute arrangements for the influencers she had hired and other invited guests.

Some reporters and influencers wanted interviews with Simon. She made all the arrangements via email, never calling him, never seeing if he was free or available to do them.

Laura emailed him when the influencers would be there, never asking if that fit into his schedule. She expected he would do it if he wanted good press.

When she did show up for the interviews, she stayed in the background, never prompting him or helping him in any way.

When he spoke to her, he barked a command or statement. She pretended she hadn't heard him or ignored him altogether.

Two days before the grand opening, Laura got an email from Kyle. Kyle asked her if she could accommodate some more guests. He wanted to invite some of the VIPs from Black Kat Investors.

He also wanted to invite Bobby Pearce from Star 1 winery to bring some of the wines that were on the menu at Buon Cibo.

Laura raised her eyebrow. Was Bobby coming to Atlanta? She'd avoided his calls and texts after she had left Napa. Their working relationship was cool, but they still emailed each other. Sometimes, rarely, they spoke on the phone. Maybe they could rekindle their sexual relationship, if only for a few days.

Laura thought back to her time with Bobby. He was a skilled lover. She liked being with him when she wasn't raging at his personality. They definitely hadn't liked each other at first. That changed one fateful day in the storage shed when they couldn't keep their hands off each other.

Suddenly, Laura grew excited to see Bobby. She knew he might be angry that she had rebuffed him. She thought she should text him, to welcome him to Atlanta and ask if he had accommodations while he was here.

Laura offered to let him stay with her if he didn't have a hotel.

Laura got a response the next day. Bobby said he was staying at the Mandarin Oriental, but he'd like to see her for dinner.

Laura said she'd make reservations at a nice restaurant, and they would also see each other at Buon Cibo's grand opening. She let him know she was glad she'd get to see him again.

In reality, Laura would be glad to see Bobby's dick again. She'd be glad to have it in her again.

Laura found herself getting excited about the grand opening. She bought a new dress that would wow Simon and Bobby. She knew how to dress well.

Laura stood in her master bedroom in front of her full-length mirror, turning this way and that.

The emerald green A-line chiffon dress had a deep V-neck, which would show off Laura's ample bust. She planned to pair it with an emerald pendant necklace, emerald stud earrings, an emerald bracelet, and an emerald ring. The necklace and the stud earrings were genuine emeralds, but the rest were good knockoffs.

She planned to wear her black hair in a chignon. She had a small gold Gucci clutch bag and pair of gold strappy Jimmy Choo sandals to round out her outfit.

Laura knew she got lucky with the late February weather. She'd be able to wear those sandals. She might be a little cold, but she hoped Bobby would warm her up later that night.

The night of the grand opening, Laura sat at a table just inside the restaurant making sure only the invited guests got in.

Fanning the Flames

"Hello, beautiful," she heard a familiar voice say.

Laura looked up to see Bobby smiling down at her. She stood up and walked around the table to give him a hug and then a quick kiss.

"Bobby! I'm so glad you could be here," Laura purred. "Your wine arrived earlier this afternoon. I'm assuming you took Kyle's jet?"

"The jet picked me up very early this morning, then we flew to Austin, and we picked up Kyle and his wife. We got here this afternoon. But I'll go home on a commercial jet. First-class, though. I think I like having a rich boss," Bobby smiled.

Laura smiled back. She liked having a rich boss, too.

"Well, welcome to Buon Cibo. As soon as I'm done checking everyone in, I'll come find you."

"Want a glass of wine while you do this?" he asked.

"Maybe a glass of prosecco."

"Coming right up."

Laura had forgotten how handsome Bobby was. His hair had gotten a little grayer, but it made him look even better. He now sported a small beard, rather than the slight goatee he'd had last summer.

His beard was still neatly trimmed, and it had some gray in it. She thought it made him look even sexier. She looked forward to feeling that fuller beard between her thighs.

Bobby returned to her small table with a flute of prosecco. She was still checking guests in, but there were sparser groups now. She would be able to leave her duties and begin mingling with the guests soon.

Bobby stood across from her and watched her work. When she looked up at him, he gave her a soft smile.

Laura took a couple of sips of her drink, checked in another couple, then stood up.

"I think I can leave my post," she said. "I'll keep watching the door, but I think most people are here. There might be a few uninvited guests, but I doubt there will be many. We did hire security at the door, just in case."

Laura picked up her prosecco, put her arm through Bobby's and began walking around the restaurant, chatting with the guests, introducing Bobby as the manager of Star 1, one of the featured wines at the restaurant.

Bobby stood by her side, sipping a Star 1 Cabernet.

Simon caught sight of Laura and Bobby arm in arm and frowned. What was she doing? Was she trying to make him jealous? Was that what this was about?

Simon walked over to the pair.

"I hope you are enjoying yourself this evening," he said to Bobby. "I'm Simon Beck, the chef and partner of this restaurant."

"Bobby Pearce," Bobby said, putting out his hand. "I'm the winery manager of Star 1. You are carrying my wine."

"Oh yes. Good wine."

Laura said nothing. She really didn't intend to speak to Simon.

"And you know Laura, I see," Simon said, looking between the pair.

"We worked together out in Napa."

"Oh, yes. I'm sure you did," Simon said, realizing in an instant that Laura and he had been lovers. "Well, enjoy yourself. We'll serve dinner in about an hour."

As Simon walked away, Bobby whispered, "What's with that guy? He's kind of rude."

"He's an ass. He bosses me around like I'm his hired help, which I certainly am not," Laura spit out. Then she smiled up at Bobby. "But I don't want to talk about him. I'm so glad you are here. Let's just enjoy the evening and our meal tonight."

Thy sat together at a two-person table, smiling at each other, enjoying a wild mushroom risotto, then their main course. Laura had veal marsala. Bobby had the ragu al cinghiale, a meat sauce of wild boar served over pappardelle pasta.

At the recommendation of the wine stewards wandering among the tables, Bobby decided to try the chianti with the wild boar sauce. Laura decided on one of Star 1's merlot wines with her meal.

Both sampled a few bites of each other's dishes. Simon, as he walked among the guests, looked over at them and grimaced, thinking they looked more like love birds than people who just "worked with each other in Napa." Their body language — Laura's hand on Bobby's arm and Bobby brushing Laura's hair from her face — let him know his suspicion was right. They had been lovers.

The dessert trays came around after the meals. Simon had made small samples of panna cotta, tortes, and cannoli. He also presented samples of lemon sorbetto and hazelnut gelato.

Fanning the Flames

Small shots of limoncello were also presented at the tables. Laura took a small torte and some hazelnut gelato. Bobby opted for the sorbetto and cannoli.

As guests began to leave, Laura gathered her clutch and turned to Bobby.

"Want to come back to my place for a nightcap?"

"We could go to my hotel for one, too. That hotel is really nice."

"Do you have a bottle of Star 1 in your room?"

"My room? I thought we'd have a nightcap in the bar, Laura."

"Oh. OK. That's fine. I can Uber home from there."

"You took Uber here? You don't have your car?"

"No. I knew I'd be drinking, so I took Uber."

"Smart. OK, let's go to the Mandarin Oriental."

Laura texted for an Uber and an SUV showed up to take them to the hotel. Laura would be sure to expense the Uber.

By the time they got there, the hotel bar was about to close. They each ordered a glass of wine and decided to drink it in Bobby's room.

They took the elevator up to the 21st floor. Kyle had put Bobby in one of the suites with a balcony. He opened the room's door and Laura walked in, enjoying what she was seeing.

Laura kicked off her gold sandals and sat on the love seat. She put her wine glass down on the small table nearby and patted the seat next to her.

Bobby walked over and sat down next to her.

"Alone at last," Laura said. She reached down to rub her right foot.

Bobby shook his head at her. "Still wearing bad footwear, I see."

"Well, I'm not trudging around a winery anymore. I can wear my nice shoes again."

"Did you throw out your boots?" he asked, referring to the boots she bought in Napa to walk around the winery. When he'd first met her, she was wearing stiletto heels much like she was wearing tonight.

"I'll have you know I still have those boots and wore them recently when I was helping Simon fix the tasting menus for some social media influencers."

"You? You cooked?" Bobby said with surprise. "I wasn't sure you could scramble an egg."

Bobby was teasing her, but his words had a bit of bite to them. Laura was puzzled.

"Is something wrong?" she asked him.

Bobby blew out his breath. "I just have to know. It's been bothering me. How many men have you slept with since me?"

"I don't think that's any…"

"How many men, Laura?" he asked, his voice turning edgy.

Laura smiled and put her hand in his lap, trying to feel his crotch. Bobby pushed her hand away.

"How many men?"

"Two," Laura lied.

"The last one was that guy at the restaurant? Simon?"

"Yes, if you must know."

"Want to know how many women I've slept with since you?"

"Dozens, I hope. Some of those newspaper gals were sweet on you."

"None. There's been no one since you."

Laura stood up and tried to pull Bobby up from the loveseat. "Well, let's go to the bedroom and make up for lost time. Help me forget anyone but you."

"No, Laura."

"No? What do you mean, no?"

"I gave you my heart and you broke it," Bobby said, his voice shaking with emotion.

"I never said I loved you. I didn't want to lie to you."

"No, you never told me you loved me. I don't think you are capable of loving a man."

Laura felt as though he'd slapped her. His words stung. She felt tears come to her eyes.

"I most certainly have loved a man, and he betrayed me" she said, her voice shaking. "He betrayed me and my family."

She was angry now. She could feel her body quaking.

"I think you'd better leave," Bobby said though gritted teeth.

"I think I'd better leave, too. I was looking forward to tonight, Bobby, but if you are going to be a bastard, I'm out."

Laura grabbed her shoes off the floor and her clutch bag from the loveseat and headed for the door. She grabbed her wine glass, drank it

Fanning the Flames

quickly and threw the glass on the floor, shattering it. She would never see Bobby again.

After another Uber ride home, she canceled the reservations she'd made for them at Bones, an exclusive steak restaurant in Buckhead. She'd had to call in a favor to get that reservation on a Friday night.

She sat on her balcony, drinking another glass of wine. She turned on a small heater like the one Simon had at his condo. She was grateful she'd bought one after seeing the one at his place.

Her feet ached and she was angry. The party certainly didn't end the way she had wanted. She probably had made Simon a little jealous. She smiled in the dark at that thought.

One glass became two and more. Laura sat and drank another bottle of wine nursing her wounded pride. Laura went to bed very drunk.

Chapter 15

Laura woke up in the early afternoon hungover. She was angry with Bobby and depressed that they hadn't gotten together. Why had he been so concerned about the men she'd slept with? It was none of his business.

She wished she'd lied to him. But he caught her completely off guard.

She shuffled into her kitchen to make her Cuban coffee. She opened her refrigerator and found her milk had gone sour. Her mood darkened. She stopped making coffee.

Laura called down to the concierge and asked if they could send up some cream or milk. Hers had gone sour. A few minutes later, her condo doorbell buzzed, and she found a small metal pitcher of milk on her doorstep.

Laura began making her coffee again. As she stirred in the sugar, she tried to decide what she would do with the rest of this truncated day. She probably ought to check her emails and monitor all the social media channels for good buzz about the grand opening. She could do all that from her condo.

She took her first sip of coffee and realized she'd need some ibuprofen to stop the pounding in her head. She headed into her bathroom and got four ibuprofen tablets. She remembered a fight she had with Bobby about taking four pills. She barked a bitter laugh. Bobby. She was suddenly sad. Sad that she was alone that day instead of with Bobby.

Fanning the Flames

Laura popped the four pills in her mouth, washed it down with her coffee, and frowned. Her head hurt, her stomach was upset, and she was still very tired.

Laura finished her coffee and she decided to go back to bed. She would not be checking emails or doing any work that day.

Laura awoke the next morning, feeling only slightly better. She still didn't feel well, but at least it was daylight and she'd work on all of the things she should have worked on the day before.

Once again, Laura fixed her Cuban coffee. She had just enough milk from the day before to make one cup.

She realized she'd have to get to the grocery store for a few things. She hated shopping for food on the weekends, though. If she could have afforded it, she would have had a personal shopper just for her food shopping.

Laura opened her laptop and began working through the emails from two days before, downloading all the media coverage of the restaurant opening, and doing screenshots of all the social media influencers accounts.

Elaine Dennis had been there and had wonderful food photos and a small write up on each dish.

Laura sent a report to Kyle, apologizing for being a day late. She didn't explain why she was late with the report, however.

After she'd done all that, she took a shower, dressed, and went to the grocery store, buying milk, a rotisserie chicken, a loaf of bread, some frozen vegetables, and a couple of potatoes, which she planned to microwave. At the last minute, she also bought some sour cream and three bottles of wine.

That should last her for the next couple of days. She didn't want to emerge from her condo for at least that long.

Laura existed in somewhat of a fog. If she was honest and self-aware, she was suffering from depression. But she wouldn't allow herself to think of herself as someone who suffered from depression.

Still, she languished in her condo, sleeping a lot and drinking even more. Sometimes she remembered to eat. She never skipped her morning coffee. That was her one anchor.

The only time she left her penthouse was to get more wine from the grocery store and more liquor from the liquor store.

Laura suddenly had a longing for mojitos, the drink of her Cuban ancestors, even though it was winter and fresh limes weren't all that fresh. The mint she bought looked limp, rather than fresh, as well.

After about a week of hiding out in her condo, Laura surfaced. She got in her Mercedes-Benz and headed to the stores. She'd heard from Kyle that Ravyn Shaw and Marc Linder had a baby.

Marc. She'd worked for him and slept with him. She'd tried to win him back last year in Napa, but he'd rebuffed her. And now he and Ravyn had a baby? What the hell?

Now Laura was glad she hadn't gotten back together with Marc. She decided she never wanted to have children.

As Laura thought about what to send, she smiled an evil smile. She'd send each of them a baby gift. She decided to send Ravyn a scale and a book on how to keep a man. She'd decided to send Marc a DNA kit.

Laura got back to her condo with her purchases but didn't have gift wrap nor the boxes to send them. She frowned. Now she'd have to go back to the stores for those items. It was too much.

She just wanted to be left alone. Laura wasn't going out again that day. Instead, she put her purchases on the table, smirking at the things she was going to send, and poured herself another large glass of wine.

In early April, Laura finally had her purchases boxed up and ready to mail. She sent the scale and book to Ravyn at her house in Buckhead. She had Marc's home address still in her phone contacts. She sent the DNA kit to Marc at his office. Laura smiled at her cleverness.

Laura continued to create public relations campaigns for Buon Cibo. She even met with Simon on occasion, but she made sure other people were around. She figured he'd be on his best behavior if he was observed by other people.

And for the first time in a long while, Laura had no man in her life. It was just her and her vibrator at night, but it left her more frustrated than satisfied.

She wandered around her condo, shifting from room to room, drinking glass after glass of wine until she was so tired, she fell asleep at night. It was not a peaceful or restful sleep.

Fanning the Flames

Laura often awoke in a cold sweat, dreams of Julio. The more she drank, the more she dreamed of him. His face swam in front of her, with a menacing sneer.

She also dreamed of Rico, including the horrible dream of him lying in the street bleeding, reaching out for her, calling her name.

April became a blur for Laura. A haze of wine and now sleepless nights. It was almost as if she was afraid to sleep. Afraid of the nightmares she would have.

By mid May, Laura began to come out of her funk. The sun shone more, and the Atlanta summer began. Also, schools were letting out for the summer, so traffic in Buckhead began to ease.

Laura kept up with her work, mostly from her home, but she was surprised by an invitation from Simon to a Memorial Day celebration. He wanted to do a big grilling event at Buon Cibo with friends and family of the restaurant. Laura was surprised she ended up on the list.

Laura was also annoyed he hadn't included her in the information about the event. But then, she was barely reaching out to him for any personal reasons.

She said she'd be there. Could she invite any influencers to be there as well?

Sure, he responded.

Laura found herself getting excited for the May 29 holiday. Schools would be out, which meant many Atlantans headed to beach holidays in Florida's Gulf Coast. Traffic wouldn't be so bad.

She drove with the car's sunroof open to Buon Cibo and parked in the lot early in the afternoon. She figured she could help with any publicity or guests that would arrive.

Laura decided to dress to the nines that afternoon. She wore a silver tank dress, with silver jewelry and silver stiletto sling-back sandals, and a crossover silver clutch.

The only color was her glossy ruby red lipstick, blood-red nail polish on her nails and toes, and a large ruby pendant. When she left her condo, she looked good, and she knew it.

The sign on the front of the restaurant door announced it was closed today for a private event. Laura said she was on the guest list and was admitted. It should have been her at the front door checking in guests.

That annoyed her, but then Simon greeted her warmly, which caught her off guard.

"You look like you've lost some weight, Laura," Simon said, concerned. "But you look delightful as usual," he pivoted, as she entered the restaurant.

Had she lost that much weight? She hadn't eaten that much in the past two months. Maybe she *had* lost weight. She smiled at Simon and said, "Thank you. A woman can never be too thin."

"Please, have a glass of wine. My staff is grilling chicken, pork chops, and burgers. Oh, and some portobello mushrooms in case you've gone vegetarian since the last time I've seen you."

Laura barked out a laugh. "Simon, it hasn't been *that* long since you've seen me."

Now Simon laughed too.

Laura was struck and how at ease she felt around Simon now. This was the Simon she liked. The easy-going Simon. Not the brash, bitter, rude, and abrasive Simon. Maybe with the restaurant opened, he was more at ease.

Laura smiled at Simon and reached for a glass of prosecco being offered by restaurant wait staff. She lifted her glass to Simon and said, "To the beginning of summer."

"To the beginning of summer," Simon repeated and nodded back.

As the afternoon progressed, more and more people showed up. Laura saw Kyle and his wife Amy.

They chatted amicably, and Kyle said he wanted to meet with Laura this week while he was in town to talk about a new client and investment he'd be announcing soon. He would need her expert public relations talent for this new client.

Laura was intrigued and pleased that he'd said expert. Maybe he was viewing her as the professional she was.

A winery, now this restaurant. The new client must be an even bigger deal. Sure, she told him. She could meet him any time this week. Kyle said he'd email her a time for a working lunch.

Laura smiled. That meant she'd get a nice lunch, for free.

Laura and Simon circled each other throughout the day. They were polite and as the day progressed, Laura could feel a little sexual tension build between them. Or was she reading the situation wrong?

Fanning the Flames

She was confused. They had ended their relationship badly. What was happening now? Was he flirting with her? Was he interested in her again? Was she interested in him again?

Simon appeared at Laura's elbow, asking, "Have you gotten enough to eat?"

"Everything I've had has been delicious. Thank you for inviting me. I wasn't sure you would."

"Oh, a party isn't a party without Laura Lucas, is it?"

Laura smiled "Well, I'm glad you think so. I'm having a lovely time."

"Would you like another drink?"

Simon pulled her by the elbow to a quiet corner of the restaurant. A waiter attempted to take her half empty glass of prosecco. Simon brushed him off and glared at him.

Instead, Simon grabbed a full bottle of prosecco. "May I refill your glass?"

"Of course."

"I've missed you, Laura," Simon said, quietly.

Laura looked up at him. In truth, she missed him, too. But she also missed a man being intimate with her. "I've missed you, too," she said softly.

"Your dress is beautiful. "It makes me want to take it off of you."

Laura smiled, but it was a sad smile.

"I'm sorry for the way it ended between us," he said. "I should never have said you were my employee. You are your own woman." Simon sighed. "It's just..."

He threw his hands up. "The pressure was getting to me," he explained. "The opening of this restaurant; my wife making demands; and you making demands."

"Demands?" Laura asked, confused.

"You said you were feeling neglected. That I wasn't paying attention to you. It's just I've never met a woman like you. So strong-willed and sure of herself. You are very intimidating."

Simon's comments almost made her laugh out loud. She was intimidating and sure of herself? She certainly didn't feel that way. Was Simon teasing her?

In the past two months, she'd been none of those things. But he hadn't seen her in her bed, depressed, only drinking coffee all day and drinking wine or liquor all night, putting herself in a stupor so she wouldn't dream, and when she did, she woke up in terror.

Simon almost looked bashful when he said, "And I should never have said those things about you and Troy. It was unkind of me."

Laura was surprised at his apology. "Well, Simon, I accept your apology if that's what this is. I'm glad we've cleared the air. I'm also sorry it ended so badly between us. I still have your watch. I'd really like for you to have it."

"I have your necklace, Laura. That was really meant for you."

"I've missed you," she said, quietly.

"I've missed you, too. My God, the night's I've lain awake thinking about you." Simon gave a deep sigh.

Just then, someone came into their corner and grabbed Simon by the elbow. Simon shrugged at Laura and let the guest lead him away from her.

Laura wandered the restaurant, making small talk with several guests, including the manager of the restaurant. She found Kyle and Amy again. She politely asked about their home in Austin, and the other investments Kyle was working on. She was curious who this big new client was.

"You won't give me a hint now?" she asked.

Kyle said he would tell her more at lunch in a couple of days. Did she know of a good restaurant where they could talk privately? Laura assured him she would email him with some suggestions.

Near early evening, Simon reappeared at Laura's side. "Don't leave without talking to me."

"OK, I'm about ready to go though. My feet are killing me."

Simon looked down. "Laura, I don't understand why you wear such shoes."

"Simon, as a man, you never have to worry about your height. I do."

Simon smiled. "Well, don't leave without talking to me, OK?"

"OK."

Simon looked around and then pulled Laura into Buon Cibo's kitchen. He kissed her in a corner while his sous chefs worked to get the last of the food out to guests, averting their eyes at their boss kissing Laura.

Fanning the Flames

Laura kissed him deeply right back. She had missed the touch of a man. She felt her panties get wet as she felt his tongue in her mouth.

"Hey, get a room!" shouted someone in the kitchen.

Simon pulled away from Laura. "Don't leave without seeing me. Promise."

Laura looked into Simon's brown eyes and repeated, "Promise."

Laura found a comfortable chair near the front of the restaurant and sat, drinking a couple more glasses of prosecco, but also asking for some sparkling water. She'd kicked off she shoes, pulling her feet under her in the chair.

As guests disappeared from the party, Simon found Laura. It was late. The restaurant was about to close. The last of the wait staff was shutting things down.

"Thanks for not leaving."

"I said I'd stay."

Simon pulled Laura from her chair and began dancing with her to the smooth jazz still playing on the piped-in music in the restaurant. Laura was hoping he wouldn't step on her bare feet, but Simon was a good dancer.

As Simon and Laura swayed to the music, Laura could feel herself getting aroused. But she wondered if she was about to be disappointed again.

"You smell so good," Simon murmured.

"You don't smell so bad yourself. Although you do smell like barbeque smoke."

Simon laughed. "Maybe I need a shower."

"Maybe you do," Laura said, her voice turning husky.

"My place is closer. And I can't wait to get you out of that dress."

"Let's go."

Laura followed Simon to his condo, parking in her familiar spot.

Simon waited for her in the lobby. They held hands as they took the elevator to his floor.

Once Simon opened the condo door, he turned to Laura and began kissing her deeply, cupping her face before pulling her zipper down from her dress. It opened but remained at her waist.

Laura returned his kisses, reaching for his pants, undoing his zipper as well.

"Let's move to the bedroom," he whispered.

He pulled Laura by the hand into the familiar room.

"Oh, Laura, I was such a fool. I've missed you," Simon whispered in her ear.

"I've missed you, too, lover. Should we shower first?"

"Shower?"

"You smell like barbecue smoke, remember?"

"Well, will you join me?"

"Just try to stop me."

Laura turned her back to Simon, who pulled her dress down, so it fell to the floor. She scooped it up and laid it across a nearby chair. Simon removed his shirt, sniffed it, and made a face. It smelled like grease and barbecue smoke. He tossed it onto his closet floor.

He then removed his pants. Dressed in just his boxers, he took Laura by the hand and led her into the bathroom. He turned on the shower, waiting until the water got warm.

Simon stood and turned the shower head to the rainwater setting. Laura unhooked her bra and pulled down her panties. Simon quickly removed his boxers and stepped into the steamy walk-in shower. Laura stepped in behind him.

Simon faced Laura, cupping her breasts. His thumbs circled her nipples, making them erect.

Laura leaned back against the shower wall. Simon stepped toward her, soaping up a plush washcloth with shower gel. He began to soap her body, finally soaping her groin.

Laura closed her eyes, enjoying the warm water, the soap suds on her body, and the heat rising inside her. She smiled when she felt Simon's erect penis touching her thigh.

Laura planted her hands on the shower wall and planted her feet, spreading her legs. Simon began rubbing the washcloth on her clit. She groaned.

"Are you ready?" he whispered.

"Yes, Simon. I'm so ready for you."

Simon put his hands on Laura's hips. He was slightly taller than Laura and wasn't sure how they were going to make love in the shower.

Fanning the Flames

Laura stood on her tiptoes, then lifted her leg, which Simon crooked over his elbow.

Simon inserted his penis, pinning Laura against the shower wall. Laura then wrapped both of her legs around Simon's hips. He thrust up into her, making Laura's back slide up against the wall with each thrust.

Her arms were around Simon's neck. The warm water rained down on them as they climaxed. After they finished, Laura sank to the floor and Simon went down to his knees, before sitting on the shower floor.

Laura turned her face up to the shower head, feeling the water on her. Simon reached behind him and turned off the water.

He got up unsteadily, his legs wobbly. Then he helped Laura to her feet. He reached for a towel and handed it to Laura. He grabbed another one for himself, toweling off in the bathroom.

Laura wrapped the towel around her and asked Simon for another one for her hair. He grabbed a third towel and Laura wrapped it like a turban around her head, her hair tucked in it.

"That was incredible," Simon said, leading Laura back into his bedroom. She sat down on his bed, toweling off her thick hair.

"I don't suppose you have a hairdryer. I hate to sleep with wet hair, and I really don't want to go home tonight."

"I don't want you to go home either, but I don't have a hairdryer. What do I need that for?" he asked, pointing to his short spiky hair. "Sorry."

"I thought maybe you had one when your daughter stays with you."

"She always brings her own."

Simon walked to his bedside table and pulled out a drawer. He pulled out a silver cross necklace.

"Here, this really belongs around your neck." He unclasped the necklace and put it once again around Laura's neck, closing the clasp.

Laura put her hand on it. "I'll bring your watch to the restaurant tomorrow."

"No rush, Laura. I'm just glad you are here now. Can you sleep on a towel, so the pillow won't get wet?"

"I'll stay up a little longer to let it dry. Do you have a T-shirt I can wear?"

"You're going to sleep in a T-shirt? I want to feel your soft skin next to mine."

"I'm just going to wear it until my hair is dry. I don't want to sit in your living room naked."

"But I'd enjoy the view better."

"Simon, a T-shirt, please. Preferably one that smells like your cologne."

He got a T-shirt from his chest of drawers, sniffed it, and handed it to her. She looked at it and realized it was a logoed shirt from the restaurant.

"Simon, you didn't tell me you ordered more logoed shirts for Buon Cibo."

"Did I need to?"

"No, but as your publicist, I should have known that. I might have been able to get you a discount."

"When I make another order, I'll let you know. We used our vendor who does all our other restaurants. I think we got a good deal. But I'll let you know when I order again."

Laura pulled it over her head and pulled on her underwear. She walked out to the living room. "It doesn't smell like your cologne," she remarked. "Any more wine left?"

Simon followed her out with a towel around his waist. "Let me," he said, reaching for some wine glasses. He pulled a Star 1 bottle of wine and poured two glasses.

"Come, sit on the couch with me."

Laura took her glass and sat next to Simon. They made small talk while finishing their wine. Then Simon refilled the glasses.

When they were done, Simon put the glasses on the kitchen countertop, took Laura by the hand, and led her back to the bedroom.

Laura sighed as she slipped under the covers and curled up next to Simon.

Chapter 16

Kyle postponed his lunch with Laura, saying he had some unexpected business back in Austin, but he'd return to Atlanta in mid-June. She should make a reservation at a restaurant where they could conduct some business.

Laura made a reservation for lunch at Bones. This time she didn't have to call in a favor since this would be lunch, not dinner on a Friday night.

She sat across from Kyle, curious about who the new client would be. What new and exciting business would she be working on?

They ordered a filet mignon for each of them, both medium-rare. Laura and Kyle decided to split sauteed mushrooms and grilled asparagus for their sides.

Kyle ordered a bottle of French Bordeaux wine for the two of them. It was on the pricier side. Laura was certainly glad she wasn't going to pay for this meal.

The waiter came with the wine, presented it to Kyle, who nodded. The waiter immediately opened it, pouring a small amount into a deep bowled wine glass and gave it to Kyle. Kyle swirled it, sniffed it and then tasted it.

Laura almost rolled her eyes at him. Was Simon rubbing off on everyone?

Kyle nodded again to accept the wine and the waiter then poured a glass for Laura, then filled the remainder of Kyle's glass.

"I know you wonder why I wanted to meet with you in person, rather than over the phone," he said.

"I love an in-person meeting if it takes place at a nice restaurant like this."

Kyle smiled. "Very well. I have a new business I'm investing in, and I want you to help launch it into a bigger profile."

"Oh, tell me more," Laura said, leaning in, her hand on her wine glass.

"Well, this is a pretty new venture for me. I want it to be a chain of automotive service stations. I'll start with just one. We don't have a name for the chain just yet. Or rather we need to rename it. But the man who will be running it is named Axel. Think of something clever with his name."

"This is a startup, right?"

"Essentially, yes. You will oversee branding. Start coming up with catchy names and a logo. I want some of your ideas a month from now. In fact, let's touch base on August 1."

"Is there a store now? The air conditioning in my Mercedes is acting up. I can bring it in. If I'm satisfied, lots of other customers will be too."

"Can't just yet. I'm buying out a guy who is retiring. He has just one shop in the Lindbergh area. You're familiar with that area?"

Laura nodded, but she rarely went there. It was mostly industrial, at least what she had seen as she'd driven through it.

"I'll start with just that one shop, I want to broaden it into more."

"You do know I'm connected to the commercial real estate industry here in Atlanta?"

Kyle looked at Laura, surprised.

"I used to work with some of those firms as clients. I can probably get the word out you will be looking for other locations."

"I'd forgotten you have that experience. That would be great. Get the word out because once the first one is open and going well, I'll want a second location."

"I'll get the word out as soon as I get home."

"Why don't you look over the purchase agreement for the first shop. It's almost complete. Maybe you'll see or know something about the property I don't."

Fanning the Flames

"Kyle, I'm not a real estate attorney. Your people should really do that."

"Don't sell yourself short, Laura. I imagine you drive a very hard bargain for anything that is important to you."

Laura thought back to the purchase of her penthouse. She did drive a hard bargain, buying below the market value from a developer trying desperately to unload it. She smiled.

"You would not be wrong."

"I knew it."

"OK. Lunch again here?" she said, hopeful.

"Sure, Laura. Bones is fine."

"Oh, we can pick somewhere else. There's Chops Lobster Bar, or Bistro Niko if you like French food."

"Let's go to Bistro Niko. I haven't been there yet. And I usually stay at the Mandarin Oriental, but Amy and I haven't eaten there yet."

"Well, when the time gets closer, I'll make reservations."

"Now that we have lunch arranged," Kyle said, irritated.

"Sorry. Tell me more about this new chain. It's automotive service stations? Like where I'd take my car?"

"Yes."

"So, like those Jiffy places?"

"No, this is where customers will get higher-end care for their cars and trucks."

"Luxury brands? Because I could work with that."

"I think at first, we will service all vehicles. We can be more exclusive once we're making money."

"Are you sure? We could probably make more money by servicing the luxury cars first."

"I'm sure, Laura. We'll start with Hondas, Fords, Mazdas, and Hyundais at first. There are far more of those on the road. Then we can move into Jaguars, Mercedes-Benz, Acura, Infiniti and others."

"Then onto the exotic cars?"

"Maybe. We'll see. Those cars need exclusive technicians. Not everyone can work on a Maserati. We won't be opening until later this year, probably. Maybe even early next year."

"Why so long?"

"We're converting it from the ground up. I'm not buying into any existing stations, just this one. Then I'll start building out new stations."

"Oh. I see."

"I need some names, ideas, and branding from you," he said, emphasizing by pointing at Laura with his fork. "By August 1."

They finished lunch, Kyle placed his AmEx Platinum Card down for the check and then Kyle walked Laura out as they waited on their vehicles from the valet.

"You know I could have picked you up today," Laura said as her black Mercedes-Benz arrived.

"I know, but I have other meetings," he said as he waited for his rental car.

"Thank you for lunch and I'll get started on my ideas."

"Bye, Laura," he said, helping her into her car.

As the summer months continued, Simon and Laura kept up their affair, but discreetly. She now came to Buon Cibo more, especially to help with influencers who continued to promote the restaurant. Some of the lesser influencers now wanted food shots.

Laura always arranged the meetings but didn't pay for any of their social media influence. The meal they got after they took their photos was payment enough.

She had renewed the contracts with several of the better influencers. Elaine Dennis, Maria Calas, and Angela Yang were asked to continue their freelance work for the restaurant. Their posts got the most shares, likes, and exposure.

When she and Simon weren't together, she worked on Kyle's new client branding, but she was having trouble coming up with a catchy name for the business.

Laura scribbled on her notepad: Axel's Motors. Axel's Car Service. Axel's Premium Car Service. Gear Check. Instant Car-ma.

Laura shoved her notes across the table. It was all garbage. She wasn't thinking creatively. Maybe what she needed was some sex with Simon. No, that would make her sleepy.

But she did want some sex.

She called Simon on his cellphone. "Can I come over tonight?"

"But you were at my place last night," he replied.

Fanning the Flames

"Simon, that was three nights ago. On Saturday. Remember?"
"Oh."
"Can I come over tonight? I'm feeling frisky."
"Laura, you are always feeling frisky."
"I haven't heard you complain yet."
Simon sighed. "Very well. Come over after closing. I should be at my place by midnight."
"I'll be there."
Laura could feel a little tingle in below her waist.

As the pair lay in bed after sex, Laura asked Simon what he knew about Kyle's new venture with the car service stations.
"What service stations?" he asked.
"He told me he's investing in a chain of car service stations. I guess just in Atlanta and right now it's just one station. He wants several, so he says. They will be from scratch. I'm to come up with a name and get the branding proposals to him in a few weeks. I'm having a serious creative block. I was kind of hoping sex would unblock me."
"Kyle has said nothing to me about a new business. I hope he still plans to keep funding our venture. If Buon Cibo is successful in its first year, we may want to open another one, maybe in that new development in Sandy Springs."
"He didn't say that he wasn't going to still be your partner. He just hired me to do this new job."
"Is that the only reason you came tonight?" Simon asked, softly. "To get yourself unblocked as you put it?"
"No. I did want to have sex with you. I wanted to be with you, Simon. I did hope that the sex would help unblock my creativity."
"And has it?"
"I'm not sure. Mostly I'm feeling sleepy now."
"Me, too. It will be an early day for me. Good night, Laura." With that, Simon rolled over in his bed. A few moments later, Laura could hear his deep, even breathing.
Despite being sleepy, Laura laid in bed for several minutes, then realized she couldn't fall asleep. She got up, got a towel from the master bathroom, and wrapped it around herself.

She then went into the kitchen to find a glass and some wine. She hoped there was still a bottle open. She didn't want to wake Simon by rummaging around his kitchen to open another one.

Laura found a bottle of white wine in the refrigerator and poured herself a generous glass. She sat on his couch, looking out through the sliding glass doors of his balcony into the night. If it wasn't so humid, she might have sat outside on the balcony.

That was the thing with the weather in Atlanta. There were only about three weeks in spring or fall when the weather was perfect. Just warm enough with little humidity.

She tucked her feet under herself and felt the cool air from the air conditioner as it kicked on and off.

Laura liked to sleep in a cool room, so she always turned her air conditioning down low in the summer when she went to bed. She didn't like to be sweaty unless she was having good sex.

Laura must have dozed off on the couch because she suddenly started and was awake. The wine glass had tipped over, emptying its contents on Simon's hardwood floors. She was grateful it hadn't shattered.

"Shit," she muttered. She took off her towel and cleaned it up as best she could in the dark. She was grateful it wasn't red wine and that Simon's condo wasn't fully carpeted.

Laura placed the glass in the sink of the kitchen and returned to the bathroom, putting the towel back on the rod.

She then crawled back under the sheet next to Simon. He stirred but did not awaken.

When she next felt him move it was early morning.

She raised her head, still sleepy from being awake most of the night, then laid her head back down. Laura pulled the covers up to her neck and rolled over, making herself into a burrito.

Simon poked her in the butt. "Get up, sleepy head. Time for me to go to work and for you to go home."

"It's too early to get up," she said, sleep in her voice. "Why don't you leave me a key? I'll lock up."

"Laura, you are just trying to get a key to my place. I told you. I don't want unannounced company, and that includes you."

Fanning the Flames

Simon could hear Laura mumbling under her breath.
"Laura, please get up. I'll make you a quick breakfast."
Laura unrolled herself from the covers. "Can I have an omelet with the truffle oil?"
"Sure."
Laura threw off the covers and sat up. She walked around the bedroom gathering her clothes, putting on her panties and her bra before putting on her blouse and pants. Her shoes were in the living room where she had kicked them off when she arrived last night.

Simon stood at the kitchen counter and whipped eggs in a bowl. He sliced some smoked gouda cheese and diced some leftover prosciutto. He started the omelet and before he turned the other half over, he laid the cheese and prosciutto inside the omelet.

Simon diced some chives as the omelet finished cooking. He plated the omelet for Laura, putting on half of the chives and drizzled some truffle oil on it. Then he began to fix his own omelet.

Laura began eating her breakfast, not waiting for Simon to finish cooking his.

When she'd finished eating, she started Simon's espresso machine. "Do you want one?"
"Yes please."
She poured the first cup and handed it to Simon. Then she fixed one for herself.
"Thanks. I thought you'd drink the first one," he said, accepting the cup.
"I'm going to have to make a double for me today. I didn't sleep well last night."
"Oh, why not?"
"I just couldn't sleep. I came out here," she said, pointing to the living room, "and sat for a while."
"I didn't hear you get up."
"You were sound asleep."
"Well, I'm sorry you didn't sleep well. Make me a second cup, too, will you?"
Laura made herself a double espresso, then made one more cup for Simon. She poured sugar and milk into her strong coffee.
"Simon," she said, "have you ever had sex outdoors?"

Simon looked surprised. "No. Have you?"

Laura smiled. "Well, yes. It's exciting. Will you consider doing it outside sometime with me?"

"Where? In the woods?"

"The woods, the park, behind a building," she rattled off. "It's summer. It won't be cold. Although sex outside in the cold can be fun, too."

"Is that what you did with your boy toy?"

"You know his name was Troy. Yes, we did it outside sometimes."

"Laura, I am a businessman and professional in this community. Not only the hospitality industry, but my Jewish community. I will not have sex with you outside. It's too risky."

"But that's the fun of it," Laura said, taking a sip from her coffee cup.

"What about ticks? The woods are full of ticks."

"I've only ever gotten one. Come on, live a little."

"Absolutely not and that's final. My naked penis will not be seen by anyone outside of my private bedroom."

Laura pouted over her coffee. "Don't be such a prude, Simon."

Simon looked irritated and unhappy after their conversation.

Simon drank the rest of his coffee, then finished his omelet. He cleared their breakfast plates and began to shoo Laura toward the front door.

"Are you trying to get rid of me?" she asked. "Because of what I asked?"

"I need to get to work, Laura. I'll talk to you later."

"I haven't even finished my coffee," she said, getting annoyed.

Simon reached into a cabinet and pulled down a travel coffee mug. He took her cup from her, poured her coffee in the travel mug, and handed it back to her.

"Fine! I'll go." Laura grabbed her handbag, went to the front door, and slammed it behind her.

Chapter 17

Once again, Laura and Simon barely spoke to each other for the next few weeks. But both were working on different projects.

He worked tirelessly at the restaurant, putting in long hours, sometimes double shifts if a manager went on summer vacation. She racked her brain to come up with ideas for Kyle's new investment.

What was wrong with her? Laura wondered. She usually could come up with dozens of ideas for a product launch. Why was this auto service center chain so difficult?

The August 1 deadline arrived, and Laura emailed her ideas to Kyle. She expected they would go over her ideas at lunch the next week.

She'd made reservations at Bistro Niko and looked forward to a good lunch. She salivated over the thought of the French onion soup and a plate of scallops.

Much to her surprise and chagrin, Kyle accepted Axel's Motors as the brand and her tentative idea for the sign and logo and said he wouldn't be able to meet her for lunch in Atlanta. Laura reluctantly canceled the reservations at Bistro Niko.

She thought about just going to the restaurant solo and charging the meal to Kyle. But in the end, she didn't. She did go to the restaurant a week later and had the soup and a Croque Monsieur. She enjoyed it with a glass of white Bordeaux.

Laura put her soup spoon in the French onion soup and enjoyed the gooey gruyere with the golden cheese crusted on the top. The broth was so rich, and the onions were thick cut. Laura could have almost made a meal of the soup.

When the sandwich arrived, it was also heavy, with more gruyere cheese, ham, and béchamel sauce. The sandwich was toasted, and Laura had to ask for a box for the uneaten half of her sandwich.

She ended up ordering a second glass of wine and lingering at her table, a table for two where she was alone. She finally signaled the waiter she was ready to pay her bill and leave.

When it came time to pay, she pulled out her own American Express, but certainly not the ritzy kind. She'd have to pay for this meal herself, but Kyle's paycheck always came on time. She wasn't late with any of her bills. For that she was thankful.

Laura got back to her condo and felt a great deal of fatigue. She put it down to the rich French lunch she had just eaten.

She went into her bedroom and, fully clothed, laid down. She woke up the next morning.

Laura was disoriented when she awoke the next day. She looked at her phone and realized she missed one call and several emails.

She quickly responded to the emails and called back the influencer, apologizing for being so tardy with her response.

Laura could not shake the fatigue she felt. She had energy first thing in the morning, but by early afternoon had to go back to bed. She knew she should be hungry but couldn't bring herself to eat. In fact, she felt quite queasy.

Maybe it was that time of the month, she thought.

Then it struck her. When was the last time she'd had her period? She'd honestly lost track.

Oh, dear God, no! She thought. I cannot be pregnant. It's impossible. Impossible!

For two days she just put the thought out of her mind, but then she worried. She finally went to a pharmacy and bought an at-home pregnancy test. It was a double kit.

She sat in her bathroom, after peeing on the stick, and waited on the toilet, not having pulled her panties up.

Fanning the Flames

If she was pregnant, she knew it was Simon's baby. This would not be good news.

At last, the pregnancy test issued its results: positive.

Laura was shocked. She just assumed she couldn't get pregnant. And yet, this test showed to her abject horror she was.

She went from shock, anger, to near euphoria, then despair. She couldn't be a mother! She didn't even like children!

Laura got off the toilet, put the pregnancy stick in her Hermes bag, and headed for Buon Cibo.

She walked straight into the kitchen and found Simon in the kitchen mentoring a sous chef.

"I need to talk to you," she said. "It's urgent."

"Laura, I'm in the middle of something. Can't it wait?"

"It cannot." She began pulling his sleeve toward his office.

"Really, Laura!" Simon said. Over his shoulder, Simon called out, "Teddy, I'll be back in a minute! Don't let that sauce burn."

When Laura closed the door to the office, Simon asked, "What is so urgent, Laura?"

Laura pulled the pregnancy stick out of her purse.

"What is this?"

"A pregnancy test."

"So?"

"I'm pregnant."

Simon's shocked face could only make a tight "oh" with his mouth.

"How?" he finally said.

"You know how," Laura said, arching her eyebrow.

"No, I mean, how? You said you were on the pill."

"Well, clearly I missed a few," she lied.

"Missed a few?"

"Well, maybe more than a few."

"You lied to me," Simon said, angry. "You said you were on the pill."

"Well, Goddammit, I wasn't," Laura shouted. "I didn't think I could get pregnant."

"And why the hell not?"

"If you must know, I had an abortion when I was a teenager. An illegal one. I was really sick after it. I thought the doctor had done something so I couldn't get pregnant again."

"A good Catholic girl like you had an abortion?" Simon smirked. "No wonder you no longer go to church."

Enraged, Laura slapped Simon across the face. "You have no idea what you are talking about."

"Well, you need to take care of this one the same way you did your other one. I don't want more children, Laura," Simon shouted. "I have a grown daughter in college. I am not going to be a father again. I'm not starting over."

"You expect me to take care of it? What about you?"

"You lied to me. I'm not responsible," Simon said, throwing his hands in the air. "And I know you aren't the mothering type. You don't want this baby either." He was pointing his finger in her face and sneering.

Laura seethed at that statement. It was true, she knew. But she didn't like a man telling her what to do.

"Well, what if I want to have this baby?"

"You will not!" he shouted. "I won't support you. I want nothing to do with it."

"Why should I pay for the abortion? You should help me out."

"Are you shaking me down? You want money from me?"

"At least half! You got me into this mess!"

"That's a lie and you know it. This is all on you. I will not pay you one dime. Kyle pays you well enough. You can pay for it. I had no idea you weren't on the pill, or I would never have slept with you."

"That's a Goddamn lie and you know it," Laura shouted. "You were perfectly happy to have your dick in my pussy."

"I am not going to be a father again. I can't have my wife finding out you are pregnant!"

"Your wife?" Laura shouted. "You mean the wife you are separated from? Just how separated are you?"

Simon wouldn't answer Laura's question. He wouldn't even look at her.

"Goddammit! Are you sleeping with her?" Laura shouted.

Laura felt sick with realization that Simon had to be back with his wife. That's why he wanted her to have an abortion.

Fanning the Flames

When Simon did look up, he had a look of righteous indignation. "Our relationship is over! I never want to see you again! I can't trust you, Laura. Now get out of my restaurant!"

Laura stormed out of the office to dead silence in the restaurant kitchen. No one made eye contact and tried to look busy. She was sure everyone had heard their shouting match.

She got back to her condo and tried to decide what she'd do next.

Laura spent the next several weeks cocooned in her condo, mostly spent sleeping in bed. She was so tired.

But on a Thursday afternoon in September, she got a call from her mother.

"Mami, what is wrong?" Laura asked, suddenly concerned by the tone in her mother's voice.

"Your father has had a heart attack," her mother cried into the phone. "He's in the hospital. Come home, Laura. I need you, Papi needs you."

"Let me check flights. I'll be home as soon as I can."

Laura hadn't seen her parents, Huberto and Carmela, for several years. Laura always meant to go visit, but Miami brought back too many bad memories for her. It reminded her of her brother's death, Julio's rape, and her subsequent abortion. And her Catholic guilt.

Laura arrived in Miami and went straight to the hospital, where she met her mother.

Huberto was scheduled to be released in two days. Laura spoke to his doctor about what care he would need once home. She then helped her mother prepare their home for him.

Huberto came home looking weak and shrunken. Not the robust man Laura remembered. She was sad to think of her parents getting older.

Huberto had long ago retired from his shoe store, but so many of his former customers and friends wanted to come by with food and good wishes for a speedy recovery, that Laura and Carmela had to put a strict five-minute limit on each guest. They didn't want those well-meaning guests to wear him out and send him back to the hospital.

Laura smiled at some of the former customers who came by to say hello to her father. She remembered them from years ago. Laura sitting in the store, the smell of leather and shoe polish all around her, and gentlemen entering the store greeting her kindly.

A couple of those former customers complimented her on her shoes. Laura smiled to herself. Maybe that's where her love of shoes had come from.

Her father had sold the store when he was ready to retire. Her parents had hoped her brother would eventually take over the business, but with Rico's death, her father had simply sold the store to his cross-town rival.

Roberto Pérez, that cross-town rival, arrived in the early afternoon the first day Huberto was home from the hospital.

Laura and Carmela could not shoo him out after five minutes. Huberto was glad to see him, and the pair talked about the shoe business for an hour.

When Roberto saw Huberto was getting sleepy, he bid the family farewell and said he'd be back next week to check on them. As he was at the door, he slipped a white envelope into Carmela's hand. "Don't let Huberto know. I know he's a proud man," Roberto said.

Carmela nodded and opened the envelope after Roberto left. Inside was one thousand dollars in crisp new one hundred dollar bills. Carmela could have wept at the generosity.

Laura looked at all the casseroles on the kitchen counter.

"Mami, where are we going to put all of these? There's no more room in the freezer."

"Let's ask the neighbors if we can store them in their freezers."

Laura went next door and knocked on the Diaz family's front door. Guillerma Diaz answered.

"Laura, I heard you were back in town," the woman said. "How is your father?"

"He's home," she said, surprised to see Guillerma. "We're trying to keep visitors to a minimum, but everyone wants to see him."

Laura remembered Guillerma from high school. She wasn't a Diaz then. She was Guillerma Alvarez. She must have married one of Miguel Diaz's sons.

"Yeah, it was that way when my Benny got hurt at work," she said, ushering Laura into the house.

"Benny?"

Fanning the Flames

"Bernardo. I married Bernardo."

Laura didn't remember a Diaz son by that name. Maybe Bernardo was a cousin of the family.

"I just wanted to ask if we could store a couple of casseroles in your freezer. The one at our house is full."

"Oh sure. I'm sure my mother-in-law won't mind. She'll probably snoop to see if they brought better casseroles to your house than to ours when Miguel died."

"Oh, I'm so sorry. I didn't know Miguel had passed away."

"Yeah, last year. That's when we moved in with Juanita."

"It's just you and your husband and Juanita? This is a big house," Laura said, looking around the house.

"Same size as yours, Laura. Well, maybe a little bigger. We added a bedroom and bathroom on the first floor several years ago. Bernardo's brother Diego and his wife and their kids live here too. If you ask me, it's too many. Lots of times I can't even hear myself think."

Laura did remember Diego. He was one of Rico's friends, so Laura was sure he was a gang member as well. Or maybe he wasn't now.

"Well, thank you. I'll run back to the house and bring some of the casseroles over. In fact, you should probably eat one. You've got a full house to feed."

"I'll help you," Guillerma said. "That way I can pay my respects to your father."

The women walked back to Laura's house and Carmela threw her arms around Guillerma.

"Thank you so much for taking some of these," Laura's mother said.

"I told Guillerma to eat one of them. I didn't realize there were so many living in the Diaz house."

"You should eat all of them," Carmela said. "I don't want the food to go to waste. It would be a sin. Just let me know what the dishes are so I can write a thank you note describing how delicious they were."

Guillerma made a brief visit to Huberto, and said, "Thank you, Señora Lucas. It was good to see you, Laura. Come over sometime for a drink. We'll catch up. I'll give you all the latest gossip on the nuns from our high school."

Laura laughed. "I would like to know whatever happened to Sister Mary Michael."

"Come over tomorrow. We'll have fun," Guillerma said, carrying several casseroles stacked on each other in her arms. Laura carried two more back to the Diaz house.

When Laura got back to her home, she asked her mother to whom Guillerma was married. She didn't remember a Diaz son named Bernardo.

"It's his illegitimate son," Carmela whispered, although no one from the other house could hear her. "Juanita nearly died of shame when he showed up on their doorstep demanding to know if Miguel was his father. One look at him and you knew he was."

"Oh. That must have been awful for Juanita. But she accepted him?"

"What choice did she have? That Miguel always had a wandering eye. I'm sure she knew he was cheating on her, telling her he was working late."

Carmela grimaced, then touched the black onyx beads of her bracelet, a talisman against the evil eye. For a good Catholic woman, Laura's mother had many superstitions.

"And Guillerma married him?"

"Oh, she's a gold digger. Miguel had to write Bernardo into his will. When he died last year, Guillerma went out and bought a new dress for the funeral!"

"Mami, I'm sure she didn't…"

Carmela waved her hand at Laura dismissively. "What would you know, since you weren't here for Miguel's funeral? I saw it all."

Laura tried not to roll her eyes at her mother. She knew she was going to have to endure more Catholic guilt on this trip home.

"I'm sorry, Mami. I've been so busy with work."

"And who do you work for? You don't have a husband you need to provide for! I want grandchildren!"

"Mami, I…"

Carmela burst into tears. "Is it too much to ask? To give an old woman some grandchildren?"

Laura bit her lip. If her mother only knew she was nearly a grandmother almost 25 years ago. And now she was pregnant again! But no. Her mother must never know.

Laura knew she'd have to make arrangements for another abortion, but she wouldn't do it while she was in Miami. She'd wait until she was back in Atlanta. She doubted she was that far along. She certainly wasn't showing, thank God.

Laura was thinking about that drink that Guillerma had offered. She'd really like one about now. Laura knew her mother had some wine in the house, but she would frown if Laura asked for a glass with dinner.

The casserole Carmela put in the oven looked like a deconstructed Cuban sandwich, with pork, ham, Swiss cheese, and even some pickles on the top.

Laura helped her father up from his recliner where he had fallen asleep and helped him sit down at the table. She placed a glass of water next to him.

"Can't I have something stronger?" he whispered hoarsely.

Laura's eyebrows shot up. Her father liked a beer now and again and he loved his Cuban cigars, but she'd never known him to ask for anything much stronger to drink. At least not when she was growing up.

"Is there anything stronger in this house? I didn't pack my flask, Papi. The TSA would have taken it away."

Huberto waved his hand toward the kitchen. "Ask your mother to make me a mojito," he said.

Laura tried to hide her surprise. Maybe she *had* been away from home for too long. Her parents were drinking mojitos now with dinner?

Laura walked into the kitchen, where her mother was pulling out the casserole. "Papi is asking for a mojito. I can make it. Where's the rum?"

Carmela made a face as if she were going to deny his request, but then she shrugged. "Only one. Might as well fix one for me and you, too."

Carmela nodded toward the cabinet and Laura found a clear unmarked bottle.

"Is this it?"

"Yes."

"Is this legal?" Laura asked, unscrewing the top and sniffing it.

"Diego gets it for us. He's such a nice boy, always looking out for us after Rico passed."

Laura frowned at the statement, but got three tall glasses down from the cabinet, then went out the kitchen's side door and brought back a handful of mint. She found a couple of key limes on the kitchen counter that were big enough and began to make the mojitos.

She sugared the rims of the glasses and made the mojitos. Laura was sure this was illegal rum. Someone had a still and made homemade hooch. She hoped she wouldn't go blind drinking it.

Carmela brought the casserole to the table and Laura brought the mojitos on a tray. She also brought two more water glasses and sat them in front of the place settings.

Laura sat and picked up the serving spoon to dish a helping for her father. Her mother's hand slapped her arm, hard, almost knocking the spoon from her hand.

"We say grace in this family!" she said. "Or have you forgotten?"

Laura put down the serving spoon and bowed her head.

Carmela intoned blessings for the food, for the hands that prepared it and thanks to the Virgin Mary for taking care of Huberto at Hermosa at Our Lady of the Saints hospital.

"Amen," Laura murmured.

"Now serve your father," Carmela commanded.

Laura picked up the serving spoon and dished out a helping to her father, then reached for her mother's plate. She put a helping on it and returned the plate to Carmela.

Then Laura spooned a helping onto her plate. She bit into the meal, and she immediately remembered all the good Cuban food she couldn't get in Atlanta.

"Mmmm. This is so good," she said. Next, she picked up her mojito and took a sip. She nearly choked on how strong the rum was, but with another sip it began to go down smoothly. Jesus, she thought, this must be more than 80 proof.

The family finished their meal. Laura and Carmela cleared the table. Carmela began to make more coffee and brought over some cookies that had been homemade. Another friend had dropped them off.

"You're not going to have to fix meals for weeks, Mami."

"I'll have to give more of it to the neighbors. I don't want any of them to go to waste."

Laura brought out the coffee cups and dessert plates to the table. Laura dropped two sugar cubes into her coffee cup as her mother poured the dark liquid into her cup. Laura reached for the cream and added it to her coffee.

Fanning the Flames

Her father and mother then did the same with their coffee. After eating their dessert, Carmela told her daughter to take her father to his chair in the living room.

"Not too late, tonight, *mi amor*," she told her husband. "I should not have let you have so many visitors today. It was too much for you."

"I won't stay up much longer. I am tired," he replied, looking sleepy. "In fact, I am going to bed. Laura, help me up the stairs."

Laura took her father's arm and helped him up the stairs and into her parents' bedroom

He sat on the bed and let out a breath. "What do you need, Papi? Can I get you some water?"

Huberto nodded his head. Laura went into the bathroom and brought back a glass of water.

He sipped it, then put it on the nightstand, next to his wife's rosary beads. Laura imagined those beads had gotten a workout when her father was in the hospital.

"Listen, I want you to promise me that if something happens to me, you will take care of your mother," he said gravely.

"Papi. Nothing is going to happen to you," she said, sitting next to him on the bed and holding his hand.

"Promise me, Laura," he said, squeezing her hand.

"I promise. I promise."

Chapter 18

Completely exhausted, Laura laid in her childhood bed long after she heard her mother get up the next morning.
Laura hadn't slept well the night before. At night her mind raced with her predicament and what she'd need to do when she got back to Atlanta.

She had texted Kyle the day before that she'd be in Miami for at least a week for a family medical emergency. She had brought her laptop and her mind began to race thinking of the work she needed to do while she was in South Florida. That exhausted her too.

As she laid awake last night, Laura could not stop thinking about Julio and Rico. When she finally did sleep, she had nightmares about both of them. She awoke in a cold sweat and hoped she hadn't called out in her sleep. She listened in the darkness but didn't hear her mother walking into the hallway.

As daylight crept into her bedroom, she could hear movement in the hallway and then heard a knock at her door.

"Yes?" she asked, sleepily.

Her mother entered her room. "Why aren't you dressed? It's Sunday. It's time for church."

"Mami, I didn't sleep well. I want to sleep in."

"I did not raise you to stay home from church. Get dressed. I'll make you some coffee. We're leaving in 20 minutes."

"Is Papi going too?"

Fanning the Flames

"Of course, he is. He is a good Catholic man."

Laura pulled the covers over her head but knew she'd have to get up and get dressed for church. She hoped she wouldn't be struck dead when she entered St. Peter & Paul Catholic Church.

Her family had been going there for as long as she could remember. She remembered going with her grandparents when they were still alive. Rico's funeral had been in the chapel and he'd been buried in the church's graveyard.

As she walked up the church's steps with her parents, she was suddenly afraid. She started to feel unwell but knew she'd just have to stick it out. She couldn't take the family car and go home.

Laura was surprised at how the Spanish mass soothed her anxiety. She caught her mother beaming at her with pride as Laura made the responses in Spanish.

Laura closed her eyes for a moment. In a flash of childhood memory, Laura remembered sitting in these same pews with her parents, Rico and her grandparents.

The pink taffeta dress she wore that day to church was itchy, especially with the white tights her grandmother Rosa insisted she wear with it. Her mother had pulled her long jet-black hair back with a wide pink ribbon that matched the dress.

Rico sat next to her father in an ill-fitting navy suit he was quickly outgrowing. If her parents insisted he wear that suit for school picture day, he'd be teased mercilessly for wearing high waters.

Laura could picture her dress and Rico's suit because there was a fading family photo in the living room. Carmela had on a floral A-line dress with a hat tilted on her head. Her father wore his best suit. Was the picture taken on Easter Sunday? Laura couldn't remember but thinking about that dress made the back of her legs itch.

Laura opened her eyes, concentrating on the mass, but squirmed in the pew thinking about that itchy dress. Her mother cut her a disapproving look.

As the elderly priest stood at the front door, greeting his parishioners as they exited, he commented on how nice it was to see Huberto. He took Laura's hand, placing his other one on top of hers.

"And who do we have here? Laura, we haven't seen you in a long time," he said.

"Sorry, padre, I'm just visiting this week," she replied in Spanish.

"More than a week. She'll be here another week," Carmela interrupted. "We'll be here next Sunday, too."

Laura didn't tell her mother she was hoping to leave on Saturday. If her father was doing well, she'd try to change her flight. She had other things to do once she got back to Atlanta. Important things.

When they got home, Laura said she wasn't feeling well and would like to go lie down.

"Don't you want some lunch?" Carmela asked.

"I must be tired from the trip and all the excitement yesterday. I'll lay down for a little while. Maybe I'll feel better after lunch."

Laura climbed the stairs slowly and got into her bedroom, before doubling over with cramping in her side and back. She felt sweat on her forehead, on the nape of her neck, and then felt clammy. Her head began to swim and she felt dizzy.

Was she running a fever? Was this food poisoning from last night's dinner? Was she having a reaction from the illegal rum she had? She didn't know. She just knew she felt awful.

Laura laid down in a fetal position, her arms wrapped around her abdomen. Suddenly, Laura felt dampness in her panties. She got up and went into the bathroom to find she was bleeding.

She sat on the toilet for a long while, trying not to cry out from the pain. She hadn't brought any menstrual pads, since she'd found out she was pregnant. Her mother was well past menopause. Laura wasn't sure what she should do.

She wadded up a small hand towel into her underwear. She'd have to get to a store to buy some feminine products.

Laura came down the stairs and asked her mother if she could borrow the car. She needed to get some maxi pads at the store.

"You look pale, Laura," her mother said, feeling her flushed cheeks. "Are you running a fever?"

"I'm not sure. Listen, I need to get those maxi pads now. It's an emergency."

Carmela handed her daughter the keys. Laura just hoped she wouldn't bleed through the hand towel and stain the driver's seat. She got to the grocery store and bought the largest size pads and box she could find.

Fanning the Flames

She went into the restroom of the grocery store and threw out the hand towel, putting on a maxi pad.

Laura drove home, contemplating stopping at the liquor store first. When she passed the second liquor store, she stopped and bought a small bottle of bourbon. When she got back in the car, she put the bottle in her handbag. It barely fit.

If she was going to miscarry, she was going to make sure she had alcohol to dull the pain.

Laura skipped lunch and dinner that day, staying in bed and making excuses to her mother that she was having "female trouble."

Carmela brought her a heating pad and a tray with toast and butter and jam.

"Try to eat something, *mija*," she said softly to her daughter. "I'll be back later for the tray and to check on you."

Carmela put her hand on Laura's. "*Te quiero.*"

"I love you, too, Mami."

Laura spent most of that night changing out her maxi pads and drinking bourbon. She wished she'd bought two boxes of the pads. She was bleeding through them at an alarming rate.

She also wished she'd purchased two bottles of bourbon. She'd have to return to both stores in the morning.

Laura's mother tapped on her daughter's bedroom door the next morning. "Laura? Are you awake?"
Laura made a muffled noise. Carmela opened the door and looked in on her daughter.
"Do you feel any better?"
"Not really. I'm having a really bad period and cramps. I wasn't due until next week, so I didn't bring anything with me," she lied. "I guess I'm early because of the stress of Papi's heart attack."
Carmela patted her daughter on the arm. "Can I do anything?"
"I need to go to the store. I need more pads."
Carmela was alarmed. "You do?"
"I should have bought a larger box."
"I can get them for you."

"No, Mami," Laura said, a little too quickly. "You need to look after Papi, just in case he gets more visitors today. I'll go. Do you need anything else at the store?"

"We have enough food to last us for weeks. But get more cream. And get some ice cream for your father. He likes chocolate chip."

"I'll get showered and go now."

Laura showered and got dressed, putting on a new pad. She got to the store, bought more pads and some cream and ice cream, then stopped at the liquor store for more bourbon. With half a bottle left from the first trip, she bought two more small bottles.

She had thought to empty her Hermes bag so she could fit the bottles inside, hoping they wouldn't clink and make her mother curious about what she had in there. She'd hide them in her room later that day.

When Laura returned home, she brought the grocery bag inside. There were two cars parked outside the front yard, so she expected her father had more visitors. She was glad she'd told her mother to stay home while she ran the errands.

Laura said hello to the visitors, then excused herself to go up to her bedroom. She turned on the heating pad and got back in bed. She took a couple more ibuprofen, downing them with a swig of bourbon. She hid the bourbon in the bottom drawer of her dresser.

The heating pad felt warm and cozy. Before she knew it, she fell asleep. Hers was not a restful sleep, however. She dreamed Julio stood before her, angry that she'd had an abortion, angry she'd gotten rid of his son and heir.

Laura never knew the sex of that aborted fetus. She tried to argue with Julio, telling him it was his fault she had to do it. In the nightmare, he began slapping her, laughing while he did so.

Laura felt a hand on her arm and screamed as she awoke. Laura's mother stood over her, worried.

"You were having a bad dream," Carmela said.

Laura could feel her heart racing. "Yes, I think I was."

"You were shouting. You were saying Julio's name."

"I was?"

"Why were you shouting the name of the man responsible for your brother's death?"

"I dreamed he was coming after me," Laura lied.

Fanning the Flames

Carmela looked at her daughter with suspicion, then sat on the bed and put her arm around her.

"I never should have let you date him. He was too old for you. He won't hurt you now," she said. "He's dead and buried. But I will give you a bracelet to ward off the evil eye."

"Mami, I'm fine."

"No, you need to wear it. He's trying to hurt this family again. His spirit is restless. He is probably in purgatory, unable to get into heaven."

Laura looked at her mother, who was entirely serious. Carmela took the onyx bracelet off her wrist and put it on her daughter's. Laura felt a chill come over her. Was Julio's spirit trying to get her?

"And I want you to go to confession."

"Why?"

"When was the last time you went to confession, Laura?"

"Ummmm," she hesitated.

"Just as I thought. You haven't been to confession. That's why Julio's spirit is haunting you. That's why the evil eye is upon you. You need to be right with God, Laura, or Julio will never leave you alone."

Laura didn't believe in the evil eye or spirits or ghosts, but she did feel haunted by Julio. Why was he in her dreams? Why did he, well, bedevil her?

"Promise me you'll go to confession."

"Ok. I'll go."

"Are you hungry? I can bring you a tray."

"No, I'll come down for dinner."

"Good. Your father is worried about you. I just told him it's womanly trouble."

"Well, it is."

"Is that all it is, Laura?"

"Of course. I'll get freshened up and come down."

Carmela nodded. She turned at the bedroom door toward Laura. "I was once young too, Laura. I know what it feels like." Then she disappeared down the hall and down the creaky stairs.

Laura sat still for a moment. What had her mother meant? Had she ever miscarried? Did she know the signs?

Laura had never asked her mother about any other children she might have had and lost. Rico was eight years older than she was.

Maybe there was a child or children that should have been born between him and Laura. Her family was Catholic after all.

She wanted to ask her mother, but those sorts of questions were never asked in her house.

Laura got up, pulled a comb through her hair, and reapplied some lipstick. She ran her hand down her blouse, trying to smooth the wrinkles.

She looked in the mirror over her dresser and sighed. She didn't look even halfway put together. She looked pale and had dark circles under her eyes.

Laura came down the stairs to see her father asleep in his recliner. She placed her hand on his shoulder. He began to stir but she rubbed his arm and moved away.

Laura found her mother in the kitchen making coffee. "Would you like a cup?" her mother asked.

"I'd love some. Maybe it will wake me up. Are there any of those cookies left?"

"Even better. Mrs. Roderiguez dropped off a key lime pie."

"Are we going to slice into it now or save it for dinner?"

Carmela waved a hand toward the man in the recliner. "Your father already had a slice before he took his nap, so I'll cut one for you."

Laura felt the tart and sweet pie dance on her tongue. She inhaled. This was what it was like to be home, to have good Cuban food whenever she wanted. Laura felt a pang of nostalgia.

"Here," her mother said, putting a cup of a hot liquid that looked the color of mud in front of her.

"But I have coffee."

"Finish your coffee and drink this."

Laura smelled it and made a face. "What is it? It smells like dirt."

"It's a tea that will make your courses regular again."

Laura looked up at her mother, who looked back at her. She knows, Laura thought to herself. Laura instantly knew her mother had experienced miscarriages herself. How many brothers and sisters would Laura have had?

"You are still looking pale," Carmela said. "I'm going to heat up the Ropa Vieja casserole tonight. You need some red meat to feed your blood."

Fanning the Flames

Laura's mouth began to water thinking of the beef, onions, garlic, peppers and tomatoes in the dish. Her mother had made it often for the family when she was a girl because there were always leftovers for the next day's lunch or dinner.

Laura tried drinking the tea, but it really did taste like dirt, earthy and muddy. She got about half of it down before she pushed the cup away.

"All of it," her mother commanded.

"Can I at least make a mojito to wash out the awful taste when I finish?"

Carmela shrugged and went out to the back garden for some mint. She also got a lime off the kitchen counter and the illegal rum from the cabinet.

Carmela began muddling the mint, dropped several teaspoons of sugar in a glass, then added the rum and fresh-squeezed lime juice.

She plopped the glass down in front of Laura. "Now finish the tea."

Laura gulped down the sludge, swallowed as fast as she could without choking, then quickly took a gulp of the mojito.

She nearly choked on its strength compared to the disgusting tea. She took a much slower sip afterward and swirled it around in her mouth.

"Thank you. This mojito is delicious."

"Don't drink it too fast."

"I won't. That rum packs a punch."

Huberto wandered into the kitchen, his thinning white hair disheveled from his nap in the recliner.

"What's going on? Did you save a slice of that pie for me?"

"You've had your slice," his wife replied. "You don't get another until after dinner."

"May I have a mojito? It's hot today," Huberto said.

"You haven't even been outside today!" Carmela exclaimed. "How would you know how hot it is?"

"It's always hot and humid here," Huberto smiled. "Fix me a mojito, *mi vida*."

Carmela sighed. Her husband knew too well how to sweet talk her.

"Do you want another one, too?" she asked Laura, who nodded.

Carmela began fixing three mojitos, placing them before her husband and daughter before sitting down at the gold-flecked gray Formica table with her own mojito.

Laura knew she'd have to sip this one slowly or she'd be drunk before dinner.

Chapter 19

Laura was beginning to feel like herself again. She was helping her mother in the kitchen and helped steady her father as he went up and down the stairs of the home. He was still weak, and he was tired at the end of the day.

Her "courses" soon stopped, and Laura had no doubt they would be regular again. She made a note to get on birth control for real when she got back to Atlanta. She was not going through this again.

Laura continued to wear the beaded onyx bracelet her mother gave her. For the first time in ages, she slept well through the night. When she awoke the next morning, she didn't quite believe the onyx got rid of the evil eye, but she'd continue to wear it for the remainder of her time at home.

Wednesday arrived and Laura's mother demanded she go to confession. Laura didn't want to go. But Carmela would not take no for an answer.

Laura decided to go to placate her mother but decided she would just make up some lesser sins and be absolved and leave within ten minutes.

Laura's mother went into the confessional first and was out within minutes. Laura couldn't imagine what her mother had to confess!

Carmela exited and nodded at Laura, who moved toward the confessional. Laura put her hand on the ornate carvings, worn down

Fanning the Flames

from years of the faithful touching them, as she entered the small wooden booth. She sat down and the priest slid the grill so he could speak to Laura.

"Welcome, my child," the priest said.

"Bless me, Father, for I have sinned," Laura intoned. "It's been several weeks since my last confession."

Laura began to sweat in the small booth and began to feel claustrophobic. She was hoping that lying in confession wasn't a bigger sin than sex with married men, unmarried sex, and any of the numerous sins she had no intention of ever confessing.

"I, I, I," Laura stammered. Overcome with grief, Laura broke down and sobbed in the confessional, collapsing over her lap, holding her waist.

"Hush, my child, hush. I am here for you. God is here for you," the priest said in a soothing voice.

"I have sinned," Laura said with great gulps. "I can't... I am sorry for these and all my sins."

Laura's sobs subsided. She felt spent.

"May almighty God have mercy on you, and having forgiven your sins, lead you to eternal life," the priest said. "Amen."

"Amen," Laura whispered.

"May the almighty and merciful Lord grant you indulgence, absolution, and remission of your sins," he said. "My child, pray the rosary for each of your sins and be helpful to your mother and father."

Laura remembered the prayer for contrition, although she hadn't said it in years. "My God, I am sorry for my sins with all my heart. In choosing to do wrong and failing to do good, I have sinned against you whom I should love above all things. I firmly intend, with your help, to do penance, to sin no more, and to avoid whatever leads me to sin. Our Savior Jesus Christ suffered and died for us. In his name, my God, have mercy."

"Amen," the priest and Laura said together. Laura automatically made the sign of the cross and exited the confessional. She fell into her awaiting mother's arms.

Laura got home and said she was tired and went straight to bed. Her head hurt, her eyes hurt, her heart hurt.

Before she got into bed, she downed two ibuprofen tablets with several fingers of bourbon. She was on the second bottle. She had to stuff the empty first bottle down in the trash so her mother wouldn't find it.

She laid in bed and tried to count how many sins she'd committed over the years. There were too many. The thoughts overwhelmed her, and she began crying again. She tried not to cry loudly. She didn't want her mother to hear her weep.

Laura finally fell asleep but didn't sleep well. Julio returned to her dreams. He was laughing at her heartache. Laughing at her sins. Laughing that she couldn't confess them to the priest.

"He'll never forgive you, Laura," Julio said to her. "No one will ever forgive you."

Laura awoke with a start. She reached for her cellphone to see what time it was. It was a little after midnight. The witching hour, Laura thought. Then she felt the onyx bracelet on her nightstand. She immediately put it on.

She sat up and quietly pulled the bourbon bottle from her dresser. Getting her glass she used for water, she poured another few fingers of the golden liquid and sipped it in the darkness of her childhood bedroom.

The ceiling fan above her bed made a soft whirring sound and she eventually put her glass down and fell back asleep.

The sunrise peeked through her bedroom curtains and woke Laura. She rolled over and stretched. She was a little hungover. She saw the empty glass on her nightstand and knew she'd better rinse that out before her mother found it and sniffed it.

Laura went into the jack-and-jill bathroom she used to share with her brother and rinsed the glass. She then hid the bourbon bottle under her blouses in the dresser.

Laura made her bed and headed downstairs. She could smell the coffee as she entered the kitchen.

"Are you feeling better, Laura?"

"I am. I slept very well."

"Did you wear your bracelet?"

"I did," she said, waving the bracelet on her right wrist.

Fanning the Flames

Carmela handed Laura a cup of coffee. A bowl of cut-up tropical fruit was on the table with several bowls and spoons.

Laura's father, who had been reading the daily newspaper in his recliner, entered the kitchen and his wife handed him a cup of coffee. He sat at the table and reached for the bowl of fruit. "*Mi amor*, is it just fruit this morning?"

"The tostada is coming," she said, standing before her fry pan.

Laura could hear the sizzle of the butter and her mouth began to water.

"Do you want some eggs?" Carmela asked.

"Yes," Huberto answered.

"Me, too," Laura said, raising a finger.

Carmela scrambled some eggs and placed them in a serving bowl. A tray of tostadas was placed next to them.

The family said grace, then filled their plates and enjoyed their breakfast. Laura found she felt a longing for this time with her family. She regretted that she'd stayed away for so long.

"More coffee?" Laura asked, getting up. "I'll have to make some more."

She began the ritual of making Cuban coffee. Laura felt calm as she did it in her parent's kitchen, looking out of the window, decorated in faded yellow half-window cafe curtains, toward the small backyard garden.

A lemon tree, a lime tree, two key lime trees, and avocado trees grew in the small backyard as well as the mint that was prolific in pots that crowded near the kitchen's side door.

At that moment, Laura knew she would email Kyle to say she would be staying another week in Miami. She would tell Kyle her father still needed her care, which was not entirely untrue.

In the evening, the family shared another of the donated casseroles and a few more mojitos.

On Saturday of that week, Carmela said it was time to clean the cemetery. Laura knew what that meant. They were going to clean the tombstone for Rico.

The morning was hot and humid, as was every Miami day in September. Laura could feel the sweat begin to build under her blouse and into her bra.

She had a spray bottle of water and a soft-bristle brush and scrubbed gently on Rico's tombstone. Laura felt it was cathartic to do this emotional labor.

Carmela let Laura clean the tombstone while she prayed the rosary over the grave.

Laura finally stood up and stretched her back. She put down the spray bottle and scrub brush and pulled off her latex gloves that her mother had insisted she wear to protect her hands.

"I miss him," Laura said.

"I do too, *mi hija*," Carmela said, dabbing her eyes. "I miss him every day. He was my beautiful boy."

"I know he was."

"I never loved you less, Laura. But I had such hopes for Rico. Your father did, too."

Laura was silent for a moment. "I know you did. You hoped he would take over the store."

"It's not just that. I wanted him to carry on the Lucas name."

"Mami, it should have been the Lopez name."

"Well, your grandfather wanted a more American name, so we are Lucas now."

"I know. And I know you wanted the Lucas name to continue. I'm sorry I couldn't give you grandchildren."

"You still can, Laura. It's not over until it's over."

"Mami, I'm not a mother like you are."

"How do you know?"

"I don't even like children."

Carmela waved her hand dismissively. "Those are other people's children. I don't like all of them either. It is different when they are your children. Your own flesh and blood."

Laura doubted it but she nodded to her mother anyway.

When the pair returned home, there was a note taped to the front door from Guillerma, asking Laura to come over to catch up over a drink.

Fanning the Flames

Carmela nodded to her daughter, who went next door and knocked on the Diaz family home's door.

A man about Laura's age answered. "We don't want no solicitors," he said, gruffly.

"I'm here to see Guillerma. I'm Laura Lucas from next door."

The man shrugged and opened the door wider. Laura followed him in.

"Sit," he commanded, pointing to an overstuffed wingback chair in the living room. "Guillerma!" he then shouted. "Someone to see you!"

"Who is it?" she shouted from somewhere upstairs.

"Laura! From next door!"

"Coming!"

Laura could hear heavy footsteps coming down the carpeted stairs. Guillerma came into the living room. "You got my note."

"If this is a bad time, I can come back. We just got back from the cemetery. We were cleaning Rico's stone."

Guillerma made a clucking sound with her tongue. "Such a shame to go so young. Come back to the kitchen. This room always reminds me of mothballs and my mother-in-law. I don't think she's had her lady friends over to visit once since Miguel died and we had the wake here."

Laura giggled, then realized she probably shouldn't have.

Guillerma waved her hand and said, "Pphtt." Then she made the sign of the evil eye.

Laura laughed. She was liking Guillerma more and more. She followed Guillerma back into the kitchen. Their houses were very similar. Laura imagined the same builder put up these homes at the same time decades ago.

'You want something to drink? A mojito?"

"I'd love one. We've been fixing them almost every night, so thank Diego for the rum."

"Do you need more? I think I've got an extra bottle."

"If you have it, I'm sure my mother would appreciate it. Where the hell does he get it?"

Guillerma took an unlabeled clear bottle down from the cabinet. "I have no idea and I don't ask. I'm sure someone is moonshining it somewhere, but you didn't hear that from me."

Lisa R. Schoolcraft

Like Laura's mother, Guillerma went out the kitchen's side door and returned with some mint and three small key limes from a tree in the backyard.

"I'd forgotten how good fresh mojitos are," Laura said as Guillerma began to muddle the mint. "Want me to juice the limes?"

"Sure. Sugar the rims of the glasses first though."

Laura took the high-ball glasses, ran them briefly under the tap, then sugared the rims from a nearby plate with sugar already on it. The Diaz family must enjoy the cocktail as much as her family.

Laura put two teaspoons of sugar in each glass, then sliced the small limes, and using the back of that teaspoon, juiced them into their glasses.

Guillerma put the mint in the glasses and poured a generous amount of rum in each.

"I'm glad all I have to do is walk home!" Laura laughed. "Salud!"

"Salud!" Guillerma repeated as they clinked glasses.

They sat down at the kitchen table, one very similar to her own family's Formica table. Only this one was deep red.

"So, tell me what you know about the nuns from our high school. I'm dying to know the gossip. Are they still around?"

"Most are dead. There's talk of closing the school because there aren't as many nuns around to teach anymore."

"I would say it's a shame, but I didn't enjoy Catholic high school, especially since it was all girls."

"The biggest scandal is what happened to Sister Mary Michael," Guillerma said conspiratorially.

"What? What happened?" Laura asked, leaning in.

"She ran off with a man!"

"At her age? Wasn't she like, in her 60s when we were going to school?"

"I think she was younger than that. She just looked older. Maybe being a nun does that. I think she was in her early 50s."

"Oh, wow. I thought she was much older."

"She met this man at bingo at the church and the next thing you know she ran off with him! Gave up her vows and married him. It was shortly after you graduated."

Fanning the Flames

"Well good for her," Laura said, banging her hand down on the tabletop. "I could never be a nun. All that praying and that vow of chastity. I like sex too much."

Guillerma giggled. "Me too."

"And shopping," Laura said, hoping she wasn't slurring her words.

"Me too! Listen we should go shopping together while you are here."

"Oh God, I'd love that! I'm going a little stir crazy with my mother in the house all the time. We can go to Louis Vuitton, Jimmy Choo," Laura said, rattling off the high-end luxury retailers.

"Please! We're not going into the stores," Guillerma said, waving her hand. "I know a place where we can get all that for cheap. Bring cash."

"You mean, a place where fashion fell off a truck?"

Guillerma laughed. "I never ask. I just get good clothes for cheap."

Laura found she was looking forward to her next adventure with Guillerma. She was two years younger than she, but she sounded fun. Why hadn't they been better friends in high school?

Then Laura realized she was so taken up with Julio, she never had time for girlfriends. Guillerma would have been a good girlfriend.

"Hey, can I ask a favor?" Laura asked.

"What is it?"

"My parents don't have Wi-Fi and I have some work I need to get done while I'm down here," Laura said. "I can pick up the Wi-Fi signal from your house. Can I use it and have the password?"

"Sure. It's easy. It's badass, one word, all uppercase."

"Badass?"

"Guess who chose the password?" Guillerma asked, rolling her eyes.

"Diego," the women said together, then burst out laughing.

The pair talked for another couple of hours, drinking another mojito. When Laura realized the time, she said she'd better be getting home and stood up from the table, swaying slightly.

"Dear God, I wonder what the proof is in this rum," she said, steadying herself by placing her hand down on the table.

"Don't know and don't care," Guillerma said, her eyes slightly glassy from the alcohol.

"Well, thanks again. This was fun. It was good to catch up. And let me know when you are going shopping. I want to come along."

"Don't forget your bottle," Guillerma said, handing the opened rum bottle to Laura.

"I hope I don't drop it on the way out," she said.

"You won't. You'll hold on tight," Guillerma said, laughing. "Don't want to have to confess the sin of smashing good booze."

Laura laughed as she stepped out of the Diaz house. She got to her front door and walked in to find her mother fixing dinner.

"Sorry, I'm so late. The time got away from me."

"Are you drunk?"

"We had a couple of mojitos. Guillerma sent over another bottle of rum for you."

Laura, with unsteady hands, placed the bottle on the table.

"Go wash your face. I don't want your father to see you drunk."

Laura went upstairs and splashed some cold water on her face. She looked in the mirror to see her eyes were glassy too, and her cheeks were flushed. She wanted to lay down in her bed and sleep.

Instead, she drew water from the tap into the glass she had been using for her nightly bourbon and gulped the cold water down. She refilled the glass and drank more water. She was going to have to pee all night, but at least she could get through dinner.

Chapter 20

Two days later Guillerma and Laura went shopping. Guillerma drove toward the industrial part of Miami and pulled up to several nondescript warehouses.

Laura could feel her anxiety begin to build as she saw them, flashing back to the warehouse where Julio had raped her.

"What's wrong?" Guillerma asked.

"Is this the right place?" Laura asked, taking several deep breaths trying to calm her racing heart.

"Of course," she said. "The best part is there is some hooch while we shop. These guys know how to keep wealthy ladies happy. You did bring cash, right?"

Laura patted her Hermes handbag in her lap.

"Oh, nice bag. Bet you can get another one here."

Laura's eyes widened. "Oh, I'd like that!"

Guillerma walked to one warehouse door, knocked, and said something in Spanish that Laura couldn't hear when the door opened a crack. Laura guessed it was some sort of password.

They walked in and Laura could not believe her eyes. Racks and racks of luxury designer clothes. Shoes lined up by size in all colors and all designers, even the stiletto heels she loved so well. And the bags! They hung on racks on the walls. She could feel her pulse quicken as she touched leather, silk and high-quality fabric.

By the time the pair left, having had several glasses of decent champagne, Laura was worried she wouldn't have enough room in her suitcase. She might have to ship some of her bounty to her Atlanta home. She didn't care. She knew she'd gotten these clothes for a steal.

Before she knew it, her trip to Miami had drawn to a close. Carmela asked Guillerma if she would drive Laura to the airport.

Huberto hadn't gotten clearance from his doctor to drive yet, and Carmela hated getting on the highway.

Guillerma had to work, but said she'd ask Diego to drive Laura to the airport. Laura declined the offer. She'd take an Uber.

As she stood outside her parents' house, waiting for the Uber to arrive, Laura found herself getting choked up at leaving. She hugged her parents hard when the driver finally arrived.

"Call us when you land, Laura," her father said.

"Come home for Christmas," her mother implored. "Be here with your family, Laura."

"Airport please," she said as the driver put her heavy bag in his trunk. Laura got in the car and put on her sunglasses. She didn't want the driver to see the tears rolling down her cheeks.

Laura was exhausted when she finally arrived at her condo. She called her mother to let her know she'd gotten home safely.

Laura undressed and began to take a long hot shower to remove the emotional stress of the past two and a half weeks.

She was behind in all of her work for the restaurant, for the winery, and now Axel's Motors. She'd tried to do some work while she was in Miami, but found she was busy most days, and too tired to get work done at night.

And the Diaz Wi-Fi was spotty. She could imagine the children on their game boxes at night making her connection weak.

She would have to start on all of it tomorrow. For tonight, she wanted a glass of wine and to go to bed.

Laura climbed into bed but could not fall asleep. Her mind whirled with the events in Miami. Her old demons were back. When she did fall asleep, she dreamed of Julio, his face menacingly close to hers. She could feel his heavy and smell his sour breath.

Fanning the Flames

She awoke with a scream, her heart racing. Why had she left that bracelet in Miami? It was her mother's bracelet after all. She'd left it on the nightstand of her bedroom. Her mother would find it when she cleaned the room.

Laura felt like the onyx was just an old wives' tale to get rid of the evil eye. Julio was dead and buried. Yet why did he continue to haunt her dreams?

Laura swung her legs over her bed. She tried to stand but found her legs wobbly. She grabbed her robe and tentatively made her way into her living room. The sun was just starting to rise in Atlanta.

She started to make coffee, already pining for the aromatic Cuban coffee her mother made each morning. Laura poured her first cup of coffee and watched the sunrise from her couch.

Laura didn't have time to waste. She worked straight through lunch to get caught up. She checked lots of emails and called Kyle to give him an update. At two o'clock in the afternoon, which was eleven in the morning in California, she emailed magazines and tourist boards to drum up more buzz for Star 1 winery.

She emailed Bobby, letting him know he might get some calls from the magazines she had contacted. She kept her emails professional. He never responded.

At eight o'clock that evening, Laura decided to quit for the day. She'd worked almost 12 hours straight. She was hungry and decided to order Chinese. She ordered kung pao chicken, extra spicy, and an order of fried dumplings and hot and sour soup.

As she waited for her delivery, she opened a bottle of pinot noir and poured a large glass. About 45 minutes later, the concierge at Laura's condo called her to let her know the food delivery had arrived and was on its way up to her penthouse.

Laura enjoyed her late dinner and enjoyed the wine even more. The bottle was nearly gone when she finished. She had more than enough leftovers for lunch the next day.

Laura decided she needed to go back to Pilates and yoga. She needed to tone up her body after her miscarriage and all of the casseroles she'd eaten in Miami.

Laura also decided to find a personal trainer to come to the house. She'd be sure to find a young male trainer and hope he'd provide some other sorts of exercise.

Three weeks later, Laura was invited to Buon Cibo for a Halloween party. She was surprised by the invitation, but she saw Kyle Quitman's name on the email invitation. It didn't come from Simon.

She rented a Wonder Woman costume, which was hard to do, given the popularity of the superhero. Her thick black hair would be perfect for the costume. Her toned body looked sexy in the unitard, and she could tighten the black patent leather belt to its lowest level. She was looking forward to letting Simon Beck see how good she looked.

And she knew she looked good. She'd worked with her trainer, Matt, twice a week for the past few weeks. He'd gotten her to limit her glasses of wine to one a night and introduced her to free weights.

He was also a massage therapist and made her sore muscles feel great. He worked out a muscle of his own in her bedroom. Laura took her new birth control prescription every day. No more unpleasant surprises.

Laura pulled up a movie poster of Wonder Woman on her laptop and copied the makeup as best she could. When she arrived at the restaurant, she saw Kyle and Amy Quitman dressed as Beauty and the Beast. Amy looked lovely in her huge yellow ball gown. Kyle, with a little stubble on his chin, had on a long blue overcoat and even had a headdress with horns.

Laura helped herself to a glass of wine as servers roamed the room with trays. Matt wasn't here to spy on her. She wouldn't tell her trainer how many she had that night.

She also ate several appetizers. They were all Italian goodies, like bruschetta, crab-stuffed mushroom caps, mozzarella rice balls, various meats and cheeses, and flatbreads.

There were also small samples of mushroom risotto, lamb lollipops, bite-sized meatballs, zucchini garlic bites, and baked ravioli. Laura was filling up fast.

She chatted with several guests, getting compliments on her costume.

Fanning the Flames

Laura turned around and caught Simon's eyes. He registered surprise at her svelte figure. She clearly wasn't pregnant.

"Laura, you are looking well," he said, hesitantly.

"I am well, thank you."

"You took care of that problem you had?" he asked.

Laura's face darkened. "I said I'd take care of it since you wouldn't help me."

Simon, dressed as a pirate, stepped closer to Laura and whispered. "I didn't like that you were attempting to blackmail me, demanding I pay for your abortion, Laura."

"You are a coward, Simon," she hissed. "A coward."

Laura's eyes narrowed as she called Simon a coward.

"I'm sorry. I was just so shocked and angry. Let me pay you half. Tell me what I owe."

Laura was about to give an outrageously large dollar amount when an older woman came up to Simon's elbow and clasped his hand.

"Your costume looks great. You really look the part," the woman said.

"Oh, Laura, allow me to introduce my wife, Rachel," Simon said, trying to make his voice sound calm and soothing.

Now it was Laura's turn to be surprised.

"Oh, your wife," she said slowly. Laura stuck her hand out. Then she grinned a little evil smile. "Well, I am Wonder Woman. I can make unwanted pregnancies disappear. Just be careful."

Rachel's mouth dropped open as she looked from Laura to Simon, uncertain. What was this woman talking about?

"Laura!" Simon said sharply. Laura could see Simon's anger flash on his face. Laura could see the utter shock on Rachel's face. "Don't even joke that way. It's not funny and completely insensitive."

Simon steered his wife away from Laura, pretending to see someone across the room, and said, "Rachel, let me introduce you to Larry Wells."

Laura left the party shortly after her encounter with Simon. She probably shouldn't have confronted him in front of his wife, but she was angry with him.

When she got to her condo, she took off her black boots, unzipped her costume and hung it up. She placed it on the back of her bedroom door. She'd return it in the next couple of days.

She scrubbed off her makeup and took off the gold bracelets and golden headpiece. Laura put on her silk pajamas.

Laura wanted to call Matt to see if they could work out horizontally that evening, but since she was more than tipsy, she decided against it. She didn't want a lecture from him about her drinking too much that night.

Laura turned on her television and flipped through the channels. Nothing caught her attention. She turned the flat screen TV off and got up. She headed to bed.

Why did Simon being with his wife bother her so? Laura sighed. She was tired of being alone. She wanted a man of her own. She finally wandered off to bed.

She managed to sleep without any violent dreams of Julio. She awoke later than she intended and saw a text message from Kyle. He wanted her to call him right away.

"Hi Kyle, what's up?" she said, when Kyle answered his cell phone.

"Why did you leave the party so early last night?"

"I was tired."

"What the hell did you say to Simon?"

Laura's heart skipped a beat. Was Kyle going to fire her? She paused before saying, "I barely spoke to him last night."

"Well, he's furious with you and has asked me to pull you off the Buon Cibo account. He doesn't want to work with you anymore."

"Why the hell not?!" Laura yelled into the phone. "Did he say why?"

"He didn't say. He just said he couldn't work with you anymore," Kyle said. "Did you sleep with him?"

Now Kyle was shouting.

"He is not your employee, which he reminded me of before we got together. You are equals."

"Laura!"

"Don't yell at me. He was separated from his wife at the time. I saw him at the party with his wife, and they are clearly back together. I guess that's why he doesn't want to work with me. Maybe I'm too tempting for him. His wife looks old."

Fanning the Flames

"Laura, you just leave scorched earth wherever you go."

"That's not true."

"Well, as you point out, he is a partner, so he can pull you off the job. You're off the job. That means I'm cutting your salary by a third, since you won't have that work to do."

"That's not fair! Look at how much I've invested in that restaurant. It had a successful launch. I've got social media influencers working on getting the buzz out. And they are *still* giving the restaurant good publicity, thanks to me!"

"Ok. But I am cutting your pay. You keep up with the social media influencers for the restaurant and work in the background. Do not contact Simon again. Keep working on the Star 1 account, too."

"Sounds to me like you want me to do the same amount of work but want to pay me less now."

"Fair point," Kyle said, his voice calmer now. "I guess that's true. I won't cut your pay, but you better deliver, and I'd better not hear any complaints from Simon."

"You won't hear any complaints from him. He's back with his wife. He won't want to confess he was with me."

"I certainly hope you are right. And Laura, you better not sleep with another one of my employees, or I *will* fire you. Do you understand?"

"Yes."

"OK. I'm glad that's settled. I'm going to have to send you a new contract with that clause in it."

"No, you don't. I understand. Before you go, when do I get to meet the guy who will be running the service station chain? I can get started on the branding and the logos. I can get them for your approval. Do I need to run them by this Axel guy as well?"

"I'll have the final approval. Send them to me."

"Well, when will I meet Axel? Can I get his input at all?"

"He has not finished his obligations."

"His obligations? What obligations are you talking about?"

Kyle sighed. "He's not out of prison yet."

"He's a fucking felon?" Laura shouted. "Oh, hell no."

"Laura, he's not just a felon. He's my stepbrother."

Laura stopped talking, shocked at what Kyle had said.

"Are you there?" Kyle asked.

"I'm still here. He's your stepbrother? So, he's Axel Quitman?"

"No. His name is Axel Lynch."

"I'm not comfortable with this."

"Why not? He's done his time. He's about to be put on parole."

"What was he in for?"

"Drugs."

"Figures."

"He'll be out soon, and he has been taking business classes in prison. I'm going to put him in charge. He's a good mechanic. That's what he was doing before he went to prison."

"If you say so."

"I do say so. And you will treat him with respect."

Laura laughed bitterly. "Well, you won't ever have to worry about me sleeping with your stepbrother."

"That's good to hear, but why not?"

"I want nothing to do with felons."

"Are you saying you won't work for him? Or me?"

"You're not the felon, Kyle. He is."

"I'm not. But Axel hasn't had it easy. And with this job, he'll stay out of trouble."

"I will work with him, but I don't have to like it or him."

"You haven't even met him, Laura. Don't judge Axel until you meet him."

"I don't need to meet him. I know his kind."

Kyle knew he couldn't argue with Laura, nor did he want to. "Work with him, Laura. Be professional, or you're fired." Kyle hung up.

Chapter 21

Laura paced her condo, angry that she was going to have to work with Axel. With Kyle threatening to fire her, what choice did she have?

But she decided she wouldn't make Axel's life easy. She knew she could be a bitch, and she was going to turn up her bitch level by 100.

Laura knew Kyle could very well fire her, so she started to send out a few emails, asking if some former clients needed her help. She was hoping she could find another marketing gig for a company, like Black Kat Investors.

In truth, she liked working for Black Kat. Kyle was a hands-off boss. He gave her a lot of autonomy to run her own schedule and run her own campaigns. Kyle was also fairly liberal with her marketing budgets.

She knew he probably questioned some of her receipts that she turned in, but he always reimbursed her. And on time.

Laura also liked that she could work from home most of the time. No clocking into an office. No filling out timesheets. She'd had enough of that when she worked for the advertising agencies years ago when she was fresh out of college.

Laura sighed. She knew she had a good job and would try to make the best of it. She would attempt to be civil to Axel, but she sure wouldn't cut him any slack. She wouldn't trust him. Not if he was a drug felon. Not if he was like Julio and Rico.

Thanksgiving came and went, and Laura's mother kept calling asking if she was returning to Miami for Christmas.

Laura finally said she would but was trying to figure out an excuse that would keep her in Atlanta.

Ironically, that excuse turned out to be Axel, who was released from prison the first week of December.

Suddenly, Laura was busy with building the Axel Motors brand, having logos designed, and working with a commercial real estate agent to renegotiate the sale in the Lindbergh area of Buckhead.

Laura faxed over the purchase agreement. She thought she'd driven a hard bargain. Kyle would certainly let her know if she hadn't.

She called her mother to say she wouldn't be able to come. Carmela cried into the phone.

"But you promised me, Laura. You promised me and your father."

"I'm sorry, Mami. This is a new client and there's a lot of work to be done. If I can break away, I will."

"One day we'll be gone, and you will regret you didn't spend time with us," Carmela said bitterly.

"Mami," Laura said, trying to soothe her mother.

"Don't Mami, me. I did not raise my daughter to be disobedient to her parents. Honor thy father and mother! You dishonor us by not caring enough to visit."

"OK, OK. I'll try to come."

"Promise me now, on your brother's grave. You will come."

"I will come," Laura heard herself promising. She hung up with her mother wondering when the Catholic guilt would end. Probably when her parents were dead and gone.

Laura shuddered. She didn't even want to think about that. When her parents were gone, she would truly be alone in the world. An orphan. No brother, nor parents.

Laura booked a flight for Miami on December 23 and a return flight for December 27. She'd be there for midnight mass on Christmas Eve and there for Christmas Day.

With this flight schedule, she'd really only be in Miami for about 72 hours with all the travel to and from the airport. If she had to promise her mother she'd be home for Christmas, she didn't have to say how long she would be staying.

Fanning the Flames

Laura forwarded the purchase agreement on the new Axel Motors to Kyle Quitman. She was hoping she'd get a small commission for all of her work. She was lucky she had some commercial real estate agencies as past clients. She knew the brokers to call.

She was also satisfied that she hadn't reached out to Craig Dawson. She didn't want him to get the commission.

Still, Craig heard about her inquiries and called her.

"Laura, why didn't you tell me you were looking for a commercial property? I could have found you a deal and given you a cut on the commission."

"Too late. Brian Robinson did that for me. And he's giving me a part of his commission."

That wasn't entirely true, Laura knew, but Craig didn't know that.

"I've missed you," Craig said.

"Are you still married?"

"Yes. But we have an agreement. Let me take you out to dinner and I can tell you all about it."

"A nice restaurant here in Buckhead?"

"Sure. Then can we go back to your place?"

"So, this is a booty call?"

Craig chuckled. "It might be."

Laura mulled over her options. She hadn't had sex in weeks after her personal trainer had quit, and she had a lot of pent-up sexual energy. She knew Craig could release that.

"Sure, Craig. Be sure to take your little blue pill before you come pick me up."

"Oh, I will Laura. I will."

Craig picked up Laura at her condo. He was driving a new blue Porsche 911 Carrera. Laura smiled when she stepped out of the lobby of her building.

Craig went around to the passenger's side and opened her door, helping her into the car.

"Is this new?" she asked when Craig got behind the wheel.

"Just got it three months ago. I helped sell a big industrial portfolio. I might make the top industrial broker for our firm this year. I thought I deserved something nice, so I bought myself a new toy."

"Well, I love your new toy," she said, running her hand along the leather seats. Craig raised a finger and then turned the seat warmers on. "Oooh! Now I really love your new toy."

"You look as lovely as ever, Laura," he said, briefly holding her hand. "I've missed you."

Laura smiled. She knew she looked good. She'd gotten a new green silk wrap dress, one that would be easy to take off this evening, and had her nails and hair done.

"Well, I wanted to look nice for you this evening. Where are you taking me?"

"I thought we'd try Noble Fin in Peachtree Corners. That way I can drive the 911 a bit more."

"Noble Fin? Peachtree Corners? I thought we were going somewhere nice in Buckhead."

"Baby, I want to drive this thing," he said, as he pushed on the accelerator. "I've heard good things about this place. Good seafood, steaks. Get whatever you want tonight."

Craig and Laura were seated, and they ordered some oysters as a starter. Laura then ordered the crab cakes, while Craig ordered a steak.

They split a bottle of merlot and skipped dessert. What they both wanted next wasn't on Noble Fin's menu.

Craig roared down Peachtree Industrial Boulevard to Buford Highway, then cut over to Georgia 400 north to get into Buckhead. He was feeling horny. Laura could tell by the way he drove fast. But then, Laura was horny too.

Craig parked his car next to Laura's Mercedes-Benz and they took the elevator up to her penthouse. When they got inside, Craig began to undo his zipper. He could feel the pressure building in his pants the entire ride home.

Next, Craig undid Laura's wrap dress. She'd worn a front-hook bra and Craig quickly undid it so he could cup her breast in his hands.

He bent down and began to lick and suck her nipples. "Oh God, I've missed these titties."

Laura reached inside his zipper and began to massage his hard cock. "Let's move to the bedroom," he murmured.

Laura was backing toward her bedroom, pulling Craig along by the waistband of his pants. She could feel herself getting wetter and wetter.

Fanning the Flames

Laura kicked off her heels and then pulled down Craig's pants. She got on her knees and put his penis in her mouth, beginning to suck hard. "Oh God, oh God," Craig moaned. He put his hands in Laura's hair and wrapped his fingers around her thick tresses. He felt his dick moving in and out of her mouth. He was afraid he was going to climax right then and there.

"Are you ready to be in me?" Laura asked, stopping the blow job.

"Yes," he whispered hoarsely.

Laura quickly got on top of her covers and pulled down her thong. Craig climbed on top of her and grabbed her by the knees, spreading her legs apart.

"Craig, I want you."

"I want in your ass."

"No. Get in my pussy."

"Fine," he said, entering her. He stroked hard inside of her. Laura could feel her orgasm begin to build.

"Oh, Craig, Craig," she moaned.

Craig suddenly pulled out and tried to have sex with her anally. Laura yelped her displeasure.

"You asshole!" she shouted. "I said no."

She pushed him off of her and rolled off the bed.

"I'm sorry, I'm sorry. It's just my wife won't let me touch her ass. We've done this before!"

"Well, not now."

"Sorry. I'll fuck you the regular way. Please, Laura. My balls are going to turn blue."

Laura reached over and pulled on Craig's penis.

"Hey! That hurt!"

"Now you know how I felt! Now get back inside me."

Craig grabbed Laura around the waist and pulled her back on the bed, got her on her back, and entered her again. He began stroking her hard. Laura could feel her orgasm begin to build again.

She opened her eyes briefly to see Craig's face all screwed up like he was about to climax.

"Come on, baby," she purred. "Harder. Harder."

"Oh, oh!" he shouted. "Laura! God! Laura!"

Laura screamed out her own orgasm. It felt deep and hard. She began to pant, unable to catch her breath.

Craig fell on top of her, then rolled over on his back. He was panting hard too.

Craig grabbed Laura's hand and squeezed it. "That was so good. I needed that. I needed you."

"It was good."

"Can I see you again?"

"You haven't stopped seeing me now. You did bring another pill, didn't you?"

"I can't take it again right now."

"But in the morning, you can take another one, right?"

"Laura, I can't stay the night. My wife…"

"I thought you said you had an agreement."

"The agreement is she doesn't ask me where I go at night."

"Oh."

Craig rolled over and pulled Laura close to him. "But I can take another pill next week. We can order in."

"I'm going to Miami to visit my parents next week for Christmas."

"Oh. Sorry to hear that."

"I'm not. I get to see my family, Craig. Now, why don't you go home and see yours?"

Soon after Craig left her condo, Laura changed her flights to Miami to extend her stay, leaving earlier than she originally planned and staying longer. She certainly didn't want to spend any of the holiday week with Craig. Maybe he'd appreciate her more if he couldn't have her for a couple of weeks.

Laura arrived in Miami and stepped out into the warm air. Atlanta had been in the low 60s, but here it was already the mid-70s. It felt good.

She exited the terminal, carrying her coat and pulling her carryon bag to wait for an Uber.

With the holiday rush, she waited longer at the airport than she expected for her rideshare, but eventually settled into the car. The driver pulled into the heavy airport traffic and got on the highway.

Laura called her mother to tell her she was on her way.

Fanning the Flames

In less than an hour, the driver pulled up to her childhood home. Her mother was on the front steps, waiting for her.

"Are you hungry? Do you want something to eat?" Carmela asked as she ushered her daughter into the house.

A live decorated Christmas tree stood in a corner of the living room and the Nativity set Laura remembered from her childhood sat on the side table that was usually behind the couch.

"Did you put that tree up all by yourself? You should have waited for me. I'd have helped."

"I wasn't sure you were coming. Diego helped me put up the tree and move the furniture."

Diego, the friendly neighborhood drug dealer and purveyor of illegal rum, Laura thought. He probably cased the place to see how expensive the TV was. But the joke was on him. Her parents still had an old TV set.

"Put your things in your bedroom and come back down for a mojito," Carmela instructed.

Laura climbed the stairs to her bedroom. She put her bag on the bed, along with her coat. The sheets were clean and fresh on her bed. She could smell the lemon scent of the sheets.

She noticed her mother's onyx bracelet lay on the nightstand. Laura quickly put it on. She wanted no bad dreams while she was home.

Laura descended the stairs and found her father in the living room in his favorite recliner. She gave him a kiss on his cheek before entering the kitchen where she found her mother making three glasses of mojitos.

"How's Papi been? His color looks good."

"He's still weak. He gets winded when we walk around the block."

"Then why do it?"

"The doctor says he needs to exercise, and he won't go to the rec center. Says there are too many kids there. He's afraid they will knock him down."

Carmela put all the glasses on a serving tray and took them out to the living room. She set the tray down and handed a glass to her husband, still in his recliner. Laura took her glass and sat on the couch. Carmela took her glass and sat next to Laura.

"So how did you get away? I thought you were too busy to come visit us."

Laura tried not to roll her eyes. "I am very busy. But it's Christmas. I wasn't going to get anything done this week anyway. A lot of people are already on vacation, since the schools are out."

"What's this new client you have? I thought you were working for that other man."

"I still work for Kyle Quitman, but he has a new venture. A chain of service stations. And his stepbrother will be in charge," Laura said. She tried to sound excited about it to her mother, who was sitting on the couch paying close attention.

"And this Kyle is married?"

"Yes. I've met his wife. She's lovely."

"Is his stepbrother married?"

"I have no idea. But I wouldn't date him anyway."

"Why not? Is he not attractive?"

"I have no idea. I haven't met him in person yet."

"Well, then how do you know? He may be very handsome and single. You could fall in love and give me a grandchild."

"Mother," Laura said, flatly. "He's a felon. He just got out of prison."

Carmela's lips pursed into a tight little line.

"I don't think you should work for him then. He might be dangerous. Why would that man ask you to work for him if he's a convict?"

"I don't like it either, but Kyle pays my salary so I can pay my bills and come visit family."

"I don't like it either," Huberto said, leaning forward in his recliner, the springs groaning. "What if he's violent? He could hurt you. Don't work with him alone. You have someone there with you. I wish your brother was still alive."

Laura frowned. Not that Rico did anything to protect her from harm while he was alive.

"We all wish Rico was here," Laura said softly.

Carmela wiped her eyes. "I miss him. I miss my baby," she croaked.

Laura patted her mother's hand. "We'll say some extra prayers for him on Christmas Eve."

Fanning the Flames

"I pray for him every day. Every day," she replied. "I don't know why God took him from me."

Tears rolled down Carmela's face. Laura could see her mother still hadn't gotten over Rico's death. But she also knew it was pointless to tell her mother Rico brought his death on himself. Either her mother truly didn't know he was a drug dealer or chose to turn a blind eye.

"Let me refresh these drinks," Laura said, putting her empty glass and her mother's half-empty glass on the serving tray. Her father quickly gulped down the rest of his drink and handed his glass to Laura.

Laura began making another round of mojitos, welcoming the break from the emotional drama in the living room. She now regretted extending her visit.

The next morning Laura awoke refreshed. She'd slept well. No night terrors. She touched the bracelet on her right wrist.

Laura could smell strong coffee brewing downstairs. The earthy aroma wafted up to her bedroom, even with the door closed.

She got up, dressed and went downstairs to the kitchen. She greeted her mother with a kiss on the cheek.

"I thought we'd go to the church today and clean Rico's grave so it will look nice for Christmas. It's a nice day today," Carmela said.

Laura thought her mother probably cleaned Rico's grave every week, but she agreed to go with her.

They got to the church cemetery and Carmela took the cleaning supplies out of her trunk. Laura guessed she just always kept them there.

Laura stood before the grave, reading Ricardo Gabriel Lucas, devoted brother and son, and giving his birthdate and the date of his death. The gravestone gleamed in the afternoon light. She put on the latex gloves her mother had given her.

Laura wished her brother had been buried near a tree for some shade as she began to spray the cleaner on the stone and gently wipe it down. She could feel the sweat begin under her bra and her cotton blouse begin to cling to her back.

She'd try to remember to ask for one of her father's old undershirts to wear the next time she came to clean the cemetery with her mother.

Laura's mother had gone back to the car and returned with some fresh-cut flowers to put in the graveside flowerpot. Carmela removed the old flowers that were dried up and withered and placed the fresh ones in the pot.

"We really should plant some flowers, Mami, so you don't have to bring new ones all the time," Laura said. "Plant a rose bush. I'll help you. They'll bloom all the time."

"No, Laura. I want Rico to have fresh flowers. My special boy deserves fresh flowers."

Carmela and Laura were quiet while Carmela arranged the flowers.

"How many miscarriages did you have?" Laura asked quietly, surprising herself by asking such an intimate question of her mother.

"Four. One before Rico and three after," Carmela replied, standing up, but still looking down at the tombstone. "Then I was pregnant with you. I was so scared I'd lose you, too. You were my miracle baby."

Carmela hugged Laura's side. "The doctors didn't think I could carry you to term. But you came out screaming at the top of your lungs. You were determined to let the world know you were here."

"Did you know about the other babies? Boys? Girls?"

"One boy ahead of Rico. The others I never knew. I didn't want to know. I just know the heartache of losing all of them. I pray for their lost souls every day."

Carmela turned to face Laura. "Your courses are back to normal?"

"Yes."

"Good. Now be a good daughter and go to confession."

"Mami…"

"Ease your mother's heart, *mi cielito*," she said. "When I get to heaven, I want to know you will join me one day."

Laura and her family went to midnight mass on Christmas Eve, then celebrated Christmas quietly together.

Laura's parents gave her a beautiful silk blouse. Laura, in turn, gave her mother the silver cross with Rico's name engraved on it. She wasn't wearing it anymore since it was a gift from Simon. Someone in her family should get good use out of it.

Her mother cried when she lifted it out of the jewelry box Laura had bought to put it in.

For her father, Laura had given a Fitbit.

"But I have a watch," he said, confused, showing Laura his left wrist.

Fanning the Flames

"It's a fitness tracker, Papi," Laura explained, now doubting the wisdom of getting her father the Fitbit. "You can track your miles, your steps, and your heart rate on your walks with Mami. And it will give you the time."

"Oh," he responded.

Laura could see the hesitancy in her father's face. "If you'd rather I get you something else, I will," she said. She had snuck away to buy him the watch after her mother said they went out walking together. She was glad she found one at the department store.

"No, this is fine. Help me put it on."

Laura took the Fitbit out of its box, setting up the time. "You just need to remember to charge it every now and again."

"It doesn't have a battery like my watch?"

"It has a rechargeable battery. I can show you how to charge it later."

She handed it back to her father, who took his old watch off and put on the new Fitbit, showing it to both Laura and his wife.

Carmela oohed and aahed over the new gadget. "That was a very thoughtful gift."

Laura knew the next time she came home the old watch would be back on her father's wrist and the Fitbit would be in a drawer somewhere.

Christmas night, Laura had trouble falling asleep. The holiday had been very emotional. She couldn't help wondering about the siblings she might have had.

If her mother had carried all those babies to term, she might have had five brothers and sisters. Christmas and this house would have been much different. Would they all have lived in this house? She couldn't imagine sharing a room with sisters.

She got up and pulled the remaining bourbon bottle from her dresser. She was glad she'd left it hidden and grateful her mother hadn't found it.

Laura poured a couple of fingers in a small glass and sipped it slowly in the dark. A tear rolled down her cheek at the thought of what might have been.

Laura stayed until the day before New Year's Eve, packing her bag and retrieving her coat from the coat closet by the front door. She stood waiting for the Uber driver.

Her mother and father hugged her hard when the rideshare driver finally arrived. Laura waved goodbye. This time, the onyx bracelet was firmly on her wrist.

Chapter 22

Laura spent a quiet night on New Year's Eve. She'd been invited to one party, but begged off, claiming she was tired from her recent trip home.

It was a quiet night by Atlanta standards. She sat out on her balcony in her heavy sweater and leggings, drinking another bottle of Star 1 Cabernet. She heard the celebratory gunfire and firecrackers at midnight.

But she wasn't ready to turn in. It was a whole new year: 2018. What would this year hold for her? she wondered.

Probably nothing different. It would likely be the same as 2017. Same work, same condo. Same everything.

Craig had left two messages on her voicemail while she was in Miami. She would call him back in a couple of days. She was giving herself New Year's Day off. After all, the other Black Kat employees had the holiday off.

Laura had to decide if Craig was a good enough lover to continue seeing him, or if she needed a new man.

Maybe she'd find someone younger, like Troy. Maybe she'd just string Craig along until she was done with him, then kick him to the curb like she'd done the last time. He'd just go back to his vanilla wife, anyway, she reasoned.

Laura was quite drunk when she finally went to bed. She still checked the security on her front door and put the empty wine bottle in her trash.

Fanning the Flames

She undressed and slipped under the covers. She loved the way the sheets felt cool against her bare skin. She shivered a bit until the down duvet warmed her.

Laura touched her wrist to make sure the onyx bracelet was still there. Then she fell asleep.

Three days later, Craig was at her condo. He had the Porsche and was ready to take her out to dinner again. This time they went to a sushi restaurant in Buckhead.

They ended up back at her place and in her bed. The next morning, Craig sent flowers and small sapphire earrings.

Laura opened the flower box to find the jewelry box. Now, this was a way to make her want to keep seeing Craig.

They continued to see each other once a week for the rest of the month.

In early February, Kyle called Laura to say the first service station was about ready to open. He'd like to set up a meeting for her to meet Axel.

"I'll set up all the publicity for the opening. Have you set a date?"

"I'm thinking about February 15. I know it's the day after Valentine's day, but it's a Thursday, so we'll have two days to get things running smoothly. Then if anything goes wrong, we'll have the weekend to do a reset."

If anything goes wrong, Laura thought, no amount of reset will overcome word of mouth. "Nothing will go wrong. But I think you should have the grand opening later in the month. I'll have a lot of work to do, even if I start right away."

"Fine. Let's make it March 1. But I want to get this project started, so no later than that. Understood?"

"Understood."

"Axel is anxious to meet you. Why don't you meet me at the service center on February 22 and we all can meet up there?"

"You don't want me to meet him alone, do you?"

"You can be intimidating, Laura."

Damn straight, Laura thought. "OK. I'll be there on February 22 at what time? Ten o'clock?"

"Meet you there."

On Thursday, February 22, Laura pulled into Axel's Motors service station in a more industrial part of Piedmont Road in the Lindbergh area.

Technically, the area was still part of Buckhead, but she didn't consider it that. The place looked low rent. The service station looked out of place by being nicer than the places immediately around it.

The sign had recently been installed and looked good. The X in Axel was an icon of two axles. The M in motors looked like pistons.

Laura was pleased with the sign and even more pleased with the graphic designer who drew up the business cards with a similar logo.

She parked along the side of the business and didn't see Kyle anywhere. She did spot a beefy man under the hood of a beat-up old pickup truck that once was red. The truck now looked faded and rusty.

She could guess the man under the hood was Axel. She couldn't see his face, but she could see his arms, covered in tattoos and very muscular.

Laura was dressed to kill, wearing her Jimmy Choo slingbacks, a tight black leather skirt, and a deep red silk blouse. Her nails were also painted blood red, and her lipstick matched.

Axel, dressed in old denim jeans with grease and oil stains and a long-sleeved black cotton shirt that was rolled up to his elbows, stood up and turned to watch her get out of her car. Laura could see he was bald.

"Hello, Axel," she said. "I'm Laura."

"I know. Kyle described you." Axel began to wipe his hands on a dirty shop rag before he stuck out his hand to shake her hand, but Laura did not stick hers out in response.

Laura could see the dirt and grease under his nails.

"Listen, I need to be very clear," she said. "I will work on your project, but I'm not happy about it."

"Why not?" Axel said, dropping his outstretched hand.

"I'm not interested in working with felons, particularly felons who are drug dealers."

Axel rocked back on his heels and folded his muscular arms across his chest.

"Is that so?"

"That is so. My brother was killed because of drugs," she said, pointing her manicured finger at Axel.

Fanning the Flames

"Well, I'm sorry to hear that. But I've done my time and paid my dues."

Just then Kyle pulled up in his rental car and got out.

"I see you two have met," he said, looking between an angry-looking Axel and an even angrier Laura.

"We've met," Axel said dryly. "I don't think Miss Lucas likes me all that much."

"Laura, I told you to treat my stepbrother with respect."

"I respectfully laid the ground rules," she responded. "Where'd you get those tattoos?" she asked Axel. "Prison? They look like gang tattoos."

"If you must know, I got these before I went to prison," Axel sneered. "These I got in prison," he said, showing her the crude ink tattoos on his fingers.

"Jesus Christ," Laura said, throwing up her hands in disgust.

"Now, Laura," Kyle said, trying to placate her. "Why don't we go inside, and we can talk about the opening next week." Kyle ushered them toward a side door into the cavernous building.

Laura grumbled something under her breath as Axel held the door for her. He smiled broadly as he caught a glimpse of her tight skirt across her ass as she walked through the door. The skirt looked as if it was painted on.

The building had a few pieces of furniture, but not much else. The service bays had all the hydraulic equipment already installed. Laura detected a faint odor of motor oil and new paint.

"Why don't we go into your office, Axel?" Kyle said.

"It's not really ready yet," Axel said. "Let's sit on the couches. Those will be more comfortable."

"You're going to have to steam clean them after you sit on them," Laura said, looking at Axel's dirty jeans.

Axel looked down at himself. "I'll go grab a shop towel."

As Axel walked toward that back, Laura yelled out, "Better make it a clean one!"

Kyle frowned. "Laura. I told you to treat Axel with respect."

"He looks like a fucking bum, Kyle, with those prison tattoos! And his hands are filthy!"

"He's clearly been working on that truck outside. Cut him some slack!"

Axel returned with a white towel and laid it across the middle of the couch, so Laura would have to sit on one side of him.

"What'd I miss? Has the princess quit yet?" Axel asked testily.

"Oh, you'd like that, wouldn't you?" Laura said, hands on hips, glaring down at the seated Axel.

"Hey, I didn't hire you. He did," Axel said, pointing to Kyle. "If it was up to me, I would not have some stuck-up broad like you anywhere near the shop."

Kyle threw up his hands in despair. "You both are acting like children fighting in the sandbox!" he said, raising his voice. "I'm not going to be your chaperone. I expect you both to act professionally to each other. Do I make myself clear?"

Axel stood up and got in Kyle's face, looking as if he was going to punch him. "Yes, boss," he sneered, then turned away.

"Laura?"

"What?"

"You are going to be on your best behavior, right?"

Laura pouted, crossing her arms.

"Laura!" Kyle bellowed.

"If I have to."

Kyle rolled his eyes toward the ceiling. He took a deep breath, trying to calm himself. "I can see this meeting isn't going to go anywhere. Laura, go home and send me all the releases ahead of the opening. You'll be here early Thursday to make sure it goes smoothly."

Kyle turned to Axel. "Be here early as well. Make sure you're cleaned up. Meeting adjourned."

Laura didn't wait to hear any more. She rushed out the side door and got in her car, peeling out of the parking lot, her tires squealing. She overshot her traffic lane and nearly hit an oncoming car.

Horns blared as she corrected and returned to her lane. Laura gripped her steering wheel hard, her knuckles turning white. She took some deep breaths to calm herself.

She quickly looked in her rearview mirror to see Axel standing outside the side door, laughing at her. She shook her head as if to clear the memory of his laughing so hard.

Laura gripped her steering wheel hard again, angry, and raised her middle finger. She wasn't sure Axel could see it, but it made her feel better. Then she sped off.

She asked herself what in God's name had she gotten herself into?

Made in the USA
Columbia, SC
29 June 2022